Prophetess

Tam DeRudder Jackson

Editor: Nikki Busch Editing
Copy Editor: Rhiannon Root
Cover Design: Steamy Designs
Formatting: Damonza
Distribution and POD: IngramSpark

Books in the Talisman Series:

Talisman
Warrior
Prophetess

For Coleene Brookshier Torgerson
You're my forever best friend. I love you.

And for everyone who's ever had a second chance.
Hope you took advantage of it.

Author's Note

Alaisdair and Shanley's story told in *Prophetess* parallels Rio and Ceri's story told in *Warrior*. It's not necessary to have read *Warrior* to enjoy this novella, but if you haven't read *Warrior* yet, perhaps after reading *Prophetess*, you'll want to read Rio and Ceri's story too.

CHAPTER ONE

Eighteen years ago, Ullapool, Scotland

SHANLEY CONLAN KNEW better.

Hamish had warned her time and time again that walking alone near dusk invited trouble. Yet, her stay in the tiny fishing village of Ullapool had been idyllic. Until today.

Walking home when Hamish didn't answer her call for a ride hadn't seemed like a big deal. In her not-so-distant university days, she'd often walked farther than the four miles separating her from her bookshop job in Ullapool and her temporary home at Conlan Manor. The setting sun painted the hillsides along the road with a broad gold brush, calming her. The setting imbued her with a peacefulness she'd had no idea she'd needed when she decided to spend a gap year at her ancestral home after graduating university. Everything about her stay in the Scottish Highlands told her she belonged there, the land and its people seeping into the marrow of her bones.

No wonder she'd let her guard down when she stopped to sniff the bright yellow gorse on the roadside. The backfire of the car slowing down alerted her. Someone needed to work on an engine.

A long-haired guy ogled her from the passenger window, and she remembered she was on the wrong side of the road. After watching the car drive out of sight around a bend, she crossed over to the right side. With a rueful shake of her head, she reminded herself to do a better job of paying attention to the traffic and driving rules practiced in the UK.

As she neared the curve in the road, an eerie quiet settled over her. Tall birch trees lined the narrow two-lane track, and she quickened her step. Before she could clear the long gentle bend, three men stepped from the trees in front of her. Recognizing one of them as the blond who'd hung out the window of the passing car, Shanley stopped.

It seemed even the natural world held its breath to see what would happen next. The breeze high in the trees died away. Birdsong halted mid-note. No furry creatures scurried amid the tall grasses and bushes interspersed through the trees.

Two dark-haired men flanked the blond, giving Shanley the idea he was their leader. The three of them together with their massive shoulders and ready stances filled up the entire road in front of her. None of them took his eyes from hers. None of them spoke. None of them looked friendly.

Trying not to panic, she took a step back.

The men stepped with her.

She knew she'd been caught out at the midway point between the village and the manor, too far in either direction to run. The trees' long shadows dropped the temperature, or maybe fear gave her the cold shivers. If only she'd mastered visualizing so she could do it without closing her eyes. Then she'd disappear, leaving these men wondering if they'd stopped to accost a woodland faerie or something.

But she hadn't mastered visualization, and she didn't dare close her eyes for the minute it would take her to see her destination inside Conlan Manor.

As each man's eyes glowed red, evil smiles stretching their lips as they revealed their true selves, her blood nearly froze in her veins.

Rogue warriors.

"Out fer an evenin' stroll, are ye lass? Does yer warrior know ye're out on yer own?" the blond asked, his tone casual, his expression menacing.

How had they found her? How did they know what she was? Shanley said nothing.

"Cat got yer tongue?" the dark-haired rogue to his left asked as he took another step toward her.

The third rogue remained silent, but she didn't miss the way he flexed his hands at his sides like he couldn't wait to put them on her.

"I can't believe Morgan has any interest in me. Even if she did, she can't take me across the ford. Unless she takes me during a battle in which my warrior is engaged. I doubt she'll be happy with the lot of you if you harm me here." She crossed her arms over her chest in a show of bravado she hoped masked the way her entire body shook.

"Yer warrior has nae idea ye're out here on yer own," the blond guessed.

"Or maybe her warrior hasnae found her yet," said the second rogue.

"Even better. After we enjoy her, maybe we can turn her so she'll help us whenever the auld witch takes it intae her head tae end our lives."

Shanley stared in horrified fascination as the blond licked his thick lips in anticipation of that idea.

Once, she'd heard that when looking imminent death in its ugly eyes, your life flashes before you in a blink. Shanley's focus telescoped down to the present moment. The birches were especially fragrant, wafting their earthy green summer scent over her.

The intense clarity of the azure sky cut into her peripheral vision. The uniform unevenness of the gravel used in the asphalt beneath her feet reminded her how thin the soles of her Chucks were.

Dear Brighid, patron goddess of stories, if you're listening, could you kindly change mine? she silently pleaded as she took another involuntary step back.

"Ye know it's nae use tae try tae outrun us. Nae matter which direction ye choose, one of us will be waitin' fer ye before ye get there," the blond rogue said, humor shimmering in his voice.

They toyed with her? Three tomcats pawing at one little mouse? She shouldn't be surprised.

"H-how did you know I'm a talisman?" she asked, stalling.

The dark-haired quiet one spoke up. "When Morgan caught up with us after we didn't find our talismans in time, she gave us a special gift. You noticed how our eyes glow red?"

"Like the evil goddess herself, or so I've been told."

"She has fire, this one," the dark-haired talkative one said.

Shanley didn't consider that a compliment.

"Get on with it," dark-and-quiet growled.

"When we come upon a woman, we can see her aura—if she has one. A talisman glows like an apricot sunset. It's even prettier in yer case with all that hair o' yers. Can't wait tae wrap it around my wrist as I take ye." The talkative one took another step in her direction.

"Remember who saw her first and who gets the first turn," blondie said, his tone turning feral as he placed a restraining hand on the other rogue's arm.

Shanley saw her chance. "Huh. Well, as you've pointed out so clearly, I have nowhere to run where you won't be waiting for me. So maybe I'd like a say in my fate. I find I rather like the tall silent type. That is if you're not going to strangle me first."

Quirking a brow at the third rogue's still flexing hands, she waited.

The man didn't change expression, but his hands relaxed. Shanley didn't.

"You don't get a say in this, woman. I saw you first, so I get the first turn," blondie insisted.

"Not if it's not what the lady wants."

Not talking much seemed to afford the third rogue some authority with the other two. Or they weren't used to him gainsaying them. Either way, at last the rogues were no longer looking at her as they stared each other down.

Shanley took a long step back, intending to gain enough distance from the men to close her eyes and visualize herself somewhere else.

Her breath backed up in her throat as a body impeded her progress.

"Ye should have waited fer me, lass," a familiar voice whispered.

She nearly dropped to the ground in relief, and probably would have if Hamish hadn't wrapped his arm around her waist to steady her.

"Now isnae the time tae lose yer head. Ye're no' safe yet," Hamish said. "Step behind me."

Shanley moved.

"What are ye about, auld man? This is not yer affair. Take yerself off before ye get hurt," the quiet rogue rumbled.

Hamish replied in Gaelic, a chant Shanley couldn't understand, but from the way the rogues' eyes widened, they had an idea.

"She's protected by a druid? He cannae dae much. Let's take him," the loud dark-haired one said as he summoned his claymore to his hand.

At the sight of the rogue's sword, she sucked in a scream.

Hamish continued to chant as the other two rogues summoned their claymores out of thin air and advanced on them. An unstoppable scream tore from Shanley's throat when she considered their imminent death at the hands of rogue warriors.

Without interrupting his chant, Hamish squeezed her hand and didn't let go.

A sudden calm overcame her, corking her screams in her throat. A golden glow enveloped first Hamish before emanating out to wrap around her. Still, the rogues advanced on them until the loud one raised his claymore to cleave Hamish in two. His blade contacted the glow with a clang, emitting a blinding spark, like static electricity run amok. He yelped in surprise and tried again while his friends surrounded them.

With gentle pressure on Shanley's arm, Hamish guided her backward. All the while, he maintained the steady rhythms of his chant. No matter how hard they tried, the rogue warriors couldn't breach the protected aura Hamish wove around Shanley and himself. She didn't question it. Instead, she moved slowly backward until they rounded the bend in the road where Hamish's car awaited them.

Instinctively, she entered the car via the driver's door. Hamish followed her inside, the aura of the chant now encompassing the car. He continued speaking as he started his battered ride and put it in gear. The rogues howled in frustration and pain as their claymores repeatedly bounced off their intended target in showers of sparks. Hamish gunned his little four-seater through the rogues and up the road, never once stinting in the chant that kept them safe. In fact, he chanted for the entire drive home and didn't stop until the two of them were safely inside the Conlan family seat.

✧

Shanley collapsed onto a hard chair at the scarred oak table in the kitchen. Sucking in air, she worked to slow her runaway heart. Hamish busied himself putting the kettle on and arranging cookies on a plate, which he set on the table beside her. A few minutes later, he set out mugs and milk and sugar. With a vague sense of unreality, she watched him as he poured boiling water over the tea in the bottom of the pot and set it on the trivet in the middle of the table to steep.

Seating himself across from her, he said nothing.

After several minutes of an uncomfortable silence Shanley had no idea how to break, Hamish said, "Would you like tae pour, or shall I?"

"My hands haven't stopped shaking enough not to make a mess."

"That certainly was a scare, lass." He splashed milk into the bottom of a mug, poured tea, and handed it to her. "One I'd rather no' repeat if ye donnae mind."

His jovial tone jerked Shanley's eyes from the teaspoon of sugar she was adding to her tea.

As she brushed the spilled sugar into a tiny pile beside her mug, he continued in the same conversational way. "What I'd like tae know is why ye couldnae wait fer me tae fetch ye."

"I'm sorry, Hamish." Using the pretense of stirring sugar into her tea, she gathered her thoughts. "The day was so beautiful. The sun shined warm for once, the sky so blue, I could swim in it. I wanted to be out in it, you know?"

"This part o' the Highlands so close tae the trainin' room at *An Teallach* draws all sorts o' warriors, no' all of 'em good guys. I warned ye about that." He grabbed a cookie, broke it in half, and dunked it in his tea.

She sighed. "It's not the same at home. I guess when one lives years of her life in relative safety, it's easy to forget how the war goddesses operate."

"I'm curious." Hamish glanced up at her from beneath his bushy white brows. "Why dinnae ye visualize yerself out o' danger when the first rogue revealed himself tae ye?"

Feeling her face heat, she looked down at the table and tightened her two-handed grip on her mug.

"I haven't mastered it yet."

"*What?*"

She put up a hand. "I can do it if I can close my eyes for a minute. But if I have to compartmentalize, keeping my eyes open to whatever danger I face and seeing in my head where I want to go, I lose focus."

Hamish thoughtfully sipped his tea. "Well, lass, since ye're so fond o' walking, I think it's time we hike tae *An Teallach* tae work on yer skills."

CHAPTER TWO

One year later

"I'M SORRY TAE see ye go, lass. Ye've been a ray o' sunshine durin' yer stay here."

"My family needs me back home," Shanley said as she stood with Hamish on the tarmac in the middle of Ullapool awaiting the arrival of the coach to Inverness.

"Yer family needs ye here as well."

Hamish's grave tone reminded her of the important protections the manor offered those who stayed in it, absorbing the layers of druidic magic associated with it.

"For whatever reason, Morgan has decided to focus her attentions on the warrior community that lives in and protects the Denver-metro area where Becca and Ian live. They have a little girl, Ceri, and Becca needs me there to help her keep my niece safe."

"I wish Becca could have brought her family over here with her," Hamish lamented.

Shanley stared into the fathomless dark chocolate eyes of her old cousin. He'd started as her teacher, but over the last year, he'd become a surrogate grandfather to her. "You know I have to go, Hamish," she said quietly.

She extended her hand to his and squeezed.

"Becca should have stayed the requisite year when she came intae possession o' the estate. That would have helped her now."

He stared across the waters of Loch Broom, his eyes even farther away.

The day of her departure was so different from the day of her arrival. When her coach dropped her off in the middle of Ullapool a year ago, clouds glowered down on the Highlands, lashing the mountains and the loch with long stinging needles of gray rain. Taranis had been in a temper that day. Shanley had wondered if the storm god resented her sister's and her presence in their family's ancestral home.

Today, the sky was so deep and crisp a blue it almost hurt her eyes to look at it. If not for the interruption of the mountains and the etchings of the wakes of fishing skiffs on the loch's smooth surface, it would have been difficult to distinguish water from sky. She thought she could swim in either—or both of them. Considering what might be awaiting her at home, she almost wished she could disappear into the rugged wild Scots landscape in front of her.

"Honestly, lass, I was rather hoping yer fate was a fine Scots warrior, one who would talk ye intae staying right here in the Highlands with us."

"The gods must have other plans."

The arrival of the coach shook her from her morose thoughts. At least if this weather held, she could anticipate a turbulence-free flight over the Atlantic. It might be nice not to have to use an airsickness bag for once. Maybe she could visualize herself home. Smiling ruefully at herself, she thought about all the training Hamish had put her through and knew without a doubt she could bend time and space and be home in Colorado before she even left Ullapool.

"That wouldnae be smart, lass. Ye know that, right?"

"I swear, Hamish I think when you were training me, you sneaked in some druid magic that lets you hear my thoughts even when I have my shield firmly in place."

"Nae. Yer eyes give ye away. That, an' I've come tae know ye well after spending so much time with ye."

He thumped the side of the coach. "Fergus here will take good care o' ye until ye reach Inverness and the first o' yer flights."

He handed her luggage to the coach driver, one of his old druid friends, who stowed it in the compartment under the bus. Hugging Shanley to him in a breath-stealing embrace, Hamish said, "Let me know when ye arrive home and safe."

Though she tried hard to hold back, the tears threatening to fall broke free, sliding in silent rivulets over her cheeks. "I'll miss you Hamish." She sniffed. "I'll miss you so much. If you ever want to come to America for a visit, you'll always be welcome."

He thumbed the tears from her face and planted a chaste kiss in the middle of her forehead.

"Take care o' yer sister and yer niece. All o' ye are precious tae our clan."

Without another word, he handed her up into the coach for the first leg of her long journey home. Funny. It felt more like she was leaving home than returning to it.

CHAPTER THREE

Two years later

"WHAT DO YOU mean, my sister is dead?" Shanley shrieked at the warrior standing at her door. Remembering her niece napping in her guest room down the hall, she lowered her voice. "You must be mistaken. Becca and Ian are on a minibreak. They weren't fighting Morgan."

"I don't know what the Rosses told you, but they were engaged in a battle."

She sagged against the doorframe.

The warrior standing on her front step was an older man, rugged and battle-tested. He reached a tentative hand to her and smoothed his fingertips along her upper arm. "I'm truly sorry, miss. But Ian's dying words to me after Morgan took your sister—"

As she choked on a sob, the warrior stared at her with sorrow-filled eyes. "He said you needed to look after the little girl. You're all she has left."

Squeezing her eyes shut, she tried to swallow over the lump in her throat as anguish overwhelmed her. Her knees gave way, and she slid bonelessly to the floor. The warrior squatted in front of her and waited.

Dropping her face into her hands, she wept. Her beautiful, vibrant, wild-child sister was gone? Forever? Becca's laughter and mischief silenced? It couldn't be real. It just couldn't.

"This is a terrible situation." The warrior paused. "But your niece needs you to be strong for her."

Sniffing back her emotions, she swiped a hand across her nose and hiccupped. "Ceri is all I have now."

"Your warrior hasn't found you yet? How old are you?"

"No," she said. "Nearly twenty-five."

He patted her shoulder. "There's still lots of time. I'll make sure to let the community know you're out here on your own with a little talisman or druid to care for. Has your family determined which your niece is?"

Knowing what the warrior did, Shanley gave him a small, grateful smile. "As far as Becca and Ian could tell, Ceri is a talisman. But druids run strong on our mother's side, so we'll have to wait a bit to know for sure."

Thinking about her mother's side of the family led to thoughts of Hamish Buchanan and Conlan Manor. Is this what he worried about? Did Becca's decision to limit her time at her Scottish manor lead to her early death? How could he know such a thing?

"Thank you for coming here. I'm sorry I made you uncomfortable."

Using the doorframe and the warrior's outstretched hand for support, she stood on shaky legs.

"You have nothing to apologize for. I'm sorry I had to bring such terrible news."

Silence stretched between them. What else was there to say? There would be no bodies, nothing to bury or scatter to the four winds. Morgan had seen to that when she waded across her river of Shanley's family's blood, leading Becca and Ian into the mists for her selfish pleasure.

"Were there others?"

"It was a setup. Twenty of us fighting a breakout of a turf war among the civilian gangs were lured into a boxed-in space in the industrial park. An army of rogues descended out of nowhere, and we had to fight our way out."

She reached out to the warrior, her turn to lend comfort.

"We lost twelve warriors and four of their talismans." He blinked at her. "It's strange, though. Once Ian and your sister went down, the fighting stopped. Abruptly." He said the last part on a whisper, like a thought had occurred to him.

"What's your name?"

"Brooks. Aemon Brooks, but everyone calls me Brooks. I'd only known your brother-in-law a short time, but damn, he was a fighter."

She gifted him a wan smile. "Thank you, Brooks, for coming here. For telling me."

"There will be a meeting in the usual place to memorialize our lost friends. I'll let you know the day." He cleared his throat. "I know the girl is young, but it's important she attends."

Shanley blew out a breath, wrapped her arms around herself, and nodded.

"My talisman suffered a similar loss when she wasn't much older than you. If you like, she can stop by, give you some advice, be an ear."

"Thanks. Please introduce us at the service."

He lifted his chin, turned, and walked slowly down the steps from her apartment. Shanley stared after him with unseeing eyes until a sound behind her yanked her attention back into the moment.

"Ceri, love. What are you doing out of bed? You still have some nap time coming."

Unblinking eyes the color of a summer meadow—the color of Becca Conlan Ross's eyes—stared back at her. "I heard you crying. Why are you crying?"

Once again, she dropped to her knees, but this time she held out her arms to her niece who walked straight into them as though Ceri meant to comfort her. Hours later, when dusk claimed the worst day of Shanley Conlan's life, Ceri slept fitfully on Shanley's lap in her double bed where they'd taken refuge from their sorrow. She ran her fingers through the silk of her niece's hair, soothing herself—and maybe Ceri too. Fresh pain flowed through her as she stared at the tracks of tears staining the angel face of her five-year-old niece. From some great distance, or perhaps only in her mind, Shanley thought she could hear the banshees wailing for the dead.

She'd gladly volunteered to babysit Ceri as Morgan amped up the pressure on the warrior community in residence in the Denver-metro area. She understood her sister and brother-in-law had an obligation to serve and protect whenever they were called upon to do so. She expected to perform the same services in the warrior community once her warrior found her, an event she reasonably thought would happen sometime during the next three years. Becca and Ian's deaths changed the scenario. Pressure to find her warrior as soon as possible to have his help in protecting not only herself, but also her niece weighed her down. She hugged Ceri close. Ceri was Shanley's whole world now.

Squeezing her eyes shut, she determined to bottle up her tears. For Ceri's sake, she needed to be strong. As twilight settled into night, she and Ceri lapsed into a restless sleep beneath the covers of Shanley's bed. When morning broke, their world remained dark.

CHAPTER FOUR

Three years later, Conlan Manor, Scotland

"SO YE MADE it home at last, lad. Good tae see ye." Hamish pulled Alaisdair Graham into a hug as he walked through the kitchen door into Conlan Manor.

"It's good tae be home. Sittin' in a bunker monitorin' the action while other warriors fought was not my cup of tea, that's fer sure. How are things here?"

Alaisdair made himself at home in the old stone kitchen in the basement of the manor. Seating himself at the battered wooden table that had served the manor's workers for generations, he waited for Hamish to put on the kettle. After stopping off to visit his parents upon his return from military service on the Continent, he'd headed directly over to visit his mentor and friend.

He'd spent his youth roaming the manor grounds and soaking up as much wisdom as he could from the old druid who took care of the place for its absentee landlady living in America. Sometimes he wondered if some sort of druid blood ran through him. When he wasn't practicing battle scenarios in the training room at *An Teallach*, his greatest pleasure lay in helping Hamish take care of the manor and grounds of the Conlan family seat. Sitting in the kitchen on a brisk autumn day gave Alaisdair a sense of peace he felt nowhere else.

"It's been quiet around here these last years without ye, lad. Though I did take on an apprentice." He set the tea things down in the middle of the table and seated himself in the chair across from Alaisdair.

"Found someone ye thought worthy o' yer skills, did ye auld man?" Alaisdair teased.

An enigmatic smile ghosted Hamish's lips. "Davy's a fine young man. Reminds me o' ye in a lot o' ways."

"Davy? Ye mean Davy Sutherland?" Alaisdair stopped pouring his tea to stare at his friend. "I thought he was a warrior." He topped up his cup, grabbed a biscuit off the tray, and sat back to await the story.

Hamish took his time to pour exactly the right amount of milk into the bottom of his mug and top it with steaming brew before he answered. "He does like sparrin' with the likes o' ye— and any other warrior he can con intae trainin' with him. But the lad is a druid, and a damn fine one. His storytellin' skills alone overmatch my own," he finished with a chuckle.

Alaisdair quirked a brow. "I find that hard tae believe. In fact, that might be the biggest story ye've told yet." He grinned as Hamish glanced up at him from beneath his bushy white brows. "The boy is what? Ten?"

"Fourteen. I'm sorry ye missed the Conlan sisters when they were here. Such bonny lasses. Which o' course they would be."

Alaisdair laughed at the change in subject, something he'd long ago become used to when it came to talking with Hamish Buchanan.

"How could they be anythin' else?" he asked innocently and hid his smile behind a sip of tea.

Hamish carried on as though Alaisdair hadn't said anything.

"The elder, Becca, was a bonded talisman with a daughter who will one day inherit the manor. Her sister, Shanley, stayed with me fer a year."

A sadness in Hamish's voice stopped Alaisdair's hand halfway to another biscuit. "The sister? Not the heir?"

"The heir dinnae understand the necessity. Her warrior's ties tae his profession and tae his community made it difficult fer him tae leave. Becca missed him and went home after only three months."

A cloud crossed his face, and Alaisdair couldn't stop himself from reaching across the table to cover the old man's hand with his own. "What happened?" he asked quietly.

Hamish stood up and walked over to the window facing the carpark at the back of the manor.

"Becca and Ian were killed by rogue warriors. The heir is now an eight-year-old orphan."

"Talisman or druid?"

"Talisman."

Alaisdair wrapped his hands around his mug. "So yer vigil continues."

"Aye, lad, it does."

∽

Following his military service to the crown, Alaisdair Graham had returned to Scotland with the singular mission of finding his talisman. To that end, he spent as many weekends as possible attending *ceilidhs* all over the Highlands, trying his sign on every woman he met. During the week, he took on the job of handyman at the manor, or rather at the cottage on the manor grounds. For some reason, Hamish insisted the old run-down stone building needed to be brought up to speed. Between refitting stones for the outer walls, resetting the flagstone floors, installing a tiny bathroom to preclude the need for running outside to use the privy, Alaisdair dragged himself into the manor each night bone weary.

The work suited him.

Yet as the weeks turned to months and his twenty-eighth birthday neared without the discovery of his talisman, his spirits plummeted. The looming possibility of a fate worse than death—serving the war goddess as one of her rogue warriors—ate at him. Somehow, he had to face the very real possibility he wouldn't find his talisman in time.

He wiped the sweat dripping from his brow as he finished installing the toilet beside the rather deceptively large shower stall. Backing out of the room, he nearly ran over Hamish.

"Damn it, man. I dinnae hear ye come in," he yelped.

He pulled the hem of his shirt up to wipe his face.

"Ye dae fine work, lad. Construction could be yer callin'—if circumstances allow."

Leave it to Hamish to address the elephant in the room head on.

"Two days, Hamish. I have two days tae find her. It's not lookin' good."

Hamish clapped him on the shoulder. "Let's take a walk, lad. Lock the door on yer way out."

It took Alaisdair awhile to figure out what the old druid was up to. Resentment flooded him before Hamish slanted him a look, not once stinting in his chanting. He hung his head in resignation before joining the druid in the protection chants he wove over and around the cottage. It seemed Hamish had anticipated Alaisdair's fate and made a contingency plan. Perhaps someday when the bitterness subsided—if he lived that long—he might even thank the old man for looking out for him.

CHAPTER FIVE

Present day

NOT FOR THE first time in the last twenty years had Shanley wished her sister could see how beautiful her daughter had grown up to be—inside and out. Ceri carried more than a little of her mother's wild child and her father's indomitable spirit. No doubt they would have been so proud of the woman she'd become.

Now the time Shanley both dreaded and anticipated was here. Today, Ceri came into her inheritance. By this time next week, she'd be thousands of miles and an ocean away, spending her required year beneath the roof of Conlan Manor. Fortunately for the clan, Becca Conlan Ross's only born had been a girl, which meant she could inherit outright and take her place as mistress of the manor. Fianna Conlan, the family's matriarch, had based the centuries-old terms of her legacy on matrilineal inheritance. Ceri was the beneficiary of Conlan Manor. Convincing her to stay for her required year would be the trick.

In honor of Ceri's pivotal twenty-fifth birthday, Shanley pulled out all the stops. If Ceri wondered at why Shanley had chosen so expensive and exclusive a restaurant for their celebration, she didn't comment.

Instead, she talked animatedly about closing her latest real estate deal and how much she missed her friend now that Alyssa Macaulay had found her warrior, taken her rightful place in the warrior community, and married on the summer solstice. Beneath the surface of their conversation simmered the knowledge that thanks to Alyssa and her new husband Rowan Sheridan, warriors now had a more level playing field on which to fight the goddesses. Shanley, at the ripe old age of forty, once again had a chance to find her warrior, something she'd given up hope for over a decade ago. Something she knew better than to hope for now.

Anyway, this moment was all about Ceri and what she needed to do for the clan's and her own protection. When dessert arrived—a hot fudge brownie with a candle on top—Shanley slid the deed to the manor across the table.

"What's this?"

"Your legacy. Now that you're twenty-five, it's time for you to take your place as mistress of Conlan Manor."

Shanley watched with bated breath as Ceri scanned the deed. Worried green eyes looked up at her.

"It's in Scotland."

"Indeed, it is."

"It says I have to reside there for a year—at least. Preferably longer."

"That's right."

"Shanley," Ceri wailed, "I can't live in Scotland. My home is here. My *business* is here." She spoke softly after a beat. "You're here."

Shanley reached across the table and covered Ceri's hand with her own, squeezing reassurance.

"You recently completed your big real estate deal, and you have nothing major on the horizon. You can lease out your townhouse. I'll come visit at Christmas, spring break, and in the summer."

"Christmas? But that's only three months away. I couldn't possibly get my act together for such a huge move by Christmas." Ceri's voice rose.

Shanley covered both of Ceri's hands with hers and stared intently into meadow-green eyes so like her late sister's. "Not only will you be celebrating Christmas at Conlan Manor, but also Thanksgiving—on your terms of course since it's not a holiday over there—and *Samhain* too."

"You make it sound like I'm leaving next week."

Shanley couldn't ignore the panic in Ceri's tone, but neither could this move wait. With a smile, she said, "You *are* leaving next week."

Ceri jerked her hands away and sat back hard against the back of her chair, looking like someone had knocked the wind out of her.

"I can't—"

"You must. Upon the occasion of her twenty-fifth birthday, the Conlan heir can waste no time returning to her ancestral home to benefit from the protections it offers her against the likes of the unholy trio of war goddesses, Maeve, Macha, and most especially, the Morrigan."

Shanley sipped her cooling coffee while she gathered her thoughts.

"You're like your mom, looking for excuses for not staying the requisite year in our ancestral estate. Of course, she had your father and you to think about, and your father insisted on staying over here. With him being the warrior, they agreed you were safer staying here with him."

A lump always invaded her throat when she thought of the beautiful light that had been her sister Becca, but she swallowed it down and continued. "After three months, Becca couldn't take the separation, and she returned home. You know what happened next."

Ceri nodded sadly while the two of them sat in silence, remembering their dead.

Shanley sucked in a breath and concluded, "I didn't have much of a plan after I finished college. On a lark, I went over to the manor for a year. Though I never found my warrior, you and I have remained safe. I can't help but think the protections of our long-ago ancestor Fianna Conlan have contributed to that happy fate."

She nodded toward the deed sitting so ominously on the table between them. "Now it's your turn to take care of family business. Who knows? Maybe your fated mate is a burly Scot who's waiting for you to arrive."

Ceri gifted Shanley with a wan smile.

With that tiny bit of encouragement, Shanley said, "Consider your year at Conlan Manor a big adventure. You can explore Scotland, immerse yourself in the culture, soak up the hauntingly beautiful atmosphere and landscape. If nothing else, you'll have all kinds of stories to tell your kids someday."

"Like the stories you've told me? Attending ceilidhs, roaming over the Highlands, getting to train in an actual training room?" Ceri lifted a skeptical brow. "You had an ulterior motive when you told those stories, didn't you?"

"Not really. That year was one of the best times of my life. I wouldn't trade it for anything."

Ceri slid the deed into her oversized leather slouchy bag. Then she picked up her spoon and finished her lovely chocolate brownie. Shanley watched her niece accept her fate and actually breathed for the first time since the two of them had sat down for their celebratory dinner. Ceri was going to Conlan Manor.

While part of Shanley had already begun mourning the loss of her niece's companionship, the part of her that loved Ceri most, felt the most pride in her, swelled with happiness and more than a little relief. The Conlan heir would return to their ancestral home and renew the protections for all the warriors, talismans, and druids connected by blood or marriage to Fianna Conlan.

CHAPTER SIX

Three weeks later

"WE'VE BEEN GLOWERIN' at me fer the better part of a quarter hour. Maybe ye want tae enlighten me about what yer problem is?" Alaisdair Graham took a sip of his tea and settled more comfortably into the cushions of the old chair he favored in Hamish Buchanan's apartment.

"Ye couldnae leave well enough alone, could ye? Ye had tae go and rush things. Now she's bringin' in some firm from America tae help her with her *prowler* problem." Hamish glared from beneath his bushy white brows.

"I live here, Hamish. This is the only home I'm ever likely tae have. Ye cannae expect me not tae use it," Alaisdair said reasonably.

"But it's no' time yet tae reveal yerself. We both know it's a long shot the fates mated ye with a talisman sixteen years yer junior," Hamish began. "And after all these years hidin' out here from the Morrigan and her minions, I understand yer eagerness. But Samhain's only a fortnight away. Surely, ye can wait that long."

Alaisdair rolled his shoulders and

deliberately stretched his legs into Hamish's space. "I wanted tae take a wee peek at the lass. Tough tae dae with ye draggin' her all over this house, chantin' and such."

Hamish quirked a brow.

"She dinnae see me, no' even once. Relax. I havnae jumped the gun."

Hamish kicked at Alaisdair's feet and stood up. "The fellow she's bringing in is a warrior." He stood at his sideboard near his herb drying table and poured a second cup of tea. "From what Ceri tells me, he's the husband of her best friend—the pair responsible fer givin' the likes o' ye this second chance at fulfillin' yer destiny. And maybe findin' a little happiness tae." He made himself comfortable in his chair once again before continuing. "I'll get the lay o' the land with this warrior before we reveal ye tae him. Which means ye should keep yerself busy in yer cottage fer the time bein' and stay out o' the manor."

Alaisdair sat forward and rested his forearms on his thighs. "I'd like tae meet this man, thank him fer putting himself in so much danger tae level the playin' field fer the rest of us. Especially those of us who went intae hiding from the community and dinnae turn rogue."

"Ye'll have plenty o' time fer that, I'm sure. But fer the sake o' the clan, ye have tae hold off on tryin' yer sign on Ceri until Samhain. That's every bit as important an event fer our family as the feat the Sheridans accomplished tae give ye the chance tae find a talisman at yer advanced age."

Hamish chortled at his joke, and Alaisdair rolled his eyes. At forty-one, he was anything but old, except in a warrior culture upended by the unholy trio a millennium ago.

Still, he didn't have much time. The old girls had only been able to steal fourteen years from warriors. Danu and the Dagda, the goddess mother and all-father of the gods and goddesses of the Celtic pantheon, gave their children opportunities even if mere mortals found those opportunities morally repugnant. In ancient times, most warriors didn't live much past the age of forty-two, so it didn't matter so much if Morgan and her sisters could steal warriors and turn them rogue late in their lives. The fact that current life expectancies were much longer didn't factor into the old equation. If he didn't find his talisman before his forty-second birthday, all chances for him would be done. He had no doubt he'd be dead within six months of that date, no matter what Hamish insisted about the Conlan protections.

His thoughts must have shown on his face as Hamish said quietly, "Have faith, boy. Ye werenae spared all these years only tae lose all hope when ye're so close. Even if Ceri isnae yer mate, yer talisman is nearby. I can feel it."

"I hope ye're right, Hamish." He sighed. "I truly hope ye're right." Standing, he stretched and walked his cup over to the sideboard. "Guess I'll turn in. See ye in the mornin'."

He let himself out of Hamish's apartment in the basement of Conlan Manor via the secret door. Motion-activated blue lights flickered on at intervals along the floor as he walked the quarter-mile tunnel to his cottage situated at the edge of the manor's grounds. Carved into the slate lying beneath the soil, the tunnel remained a steady, cool, slightly damp temperature. After the warmth of Hamish's rooms, Alaisdair shivered and turtled his neck deeper into his cable-knit sweater. Someday, he thought, it would be nice to make this walk outside—or maybe not have to make it all. Maybe he could retire to the master suite in the manor and enjoy the warmth and comfort of a beautiful woman predisposed to love him and only him as they worked together to keep evil from overtaking the world.

At that thought, his usual optimism returned, his step lightened, and he softly whistled a jolly strathspey as he strolled to his cottage.

❧

Shanley had another one of her premonitions. It had been a long time since she'd had one, but after Ceri left for Scotland, they'd started up again. This latest one left her ill. In it she witnessed a heavily muscled, auburn-haired warrior battling a horde of rogue warriors. As in previous experiences, even the ones she'd had in her twenties when she still had hopes of finding her mate, she tried to call out to him, but he couldn't hear her. The warrior fought the rogues valiantly, but he always stumbled, always went down.

She could never see the outcome, so she hoped he survived the attacks somehow. After she'd stopped experiencing the premonitions somewhere in her early thirties, she'd mourned the loss of the man she'd thought might have been her fated mate, who, of course, could no longer be living. Unless he'd become a rogue himself and somehow managed to survive without regular access to a training room and warriors with whom to train, a thought she refused to entertain. No way could she have been fated to a man who lacked character—she hoped.

Now she wondered if her premonitions were about Ceri's warrior. Perhaps her niece was on the verge of finding him. That would explain why Shanley could never communicate with the warrior she desperately wanted to help.

The day dawned gray and threatened more snow, which didn't improve her mood. The first big dump of the season already required her to awaken earlier so she could take her time driving the icy streets to her job teaching history at the local high school. Waking in a rush as a premonition assailed her left her tired and out of sorts. She jumped nearly a foot when the phone rang precisely as she headed out the door for work.

"Do you have a minute?"

Ceri's worried voice sounded like she stood right next door rather than half a world away.

"Is everything okay? Hamish isn't giving you a hard time, is he?" Shanley set her purse and briefcase down, closed her front door, and waited.

"Hamish is great. You were right about him. The issue is Rio."

"Oh dear. I worried about the two of you together when you told me he flew over to help with your security system. It's too bad Rowan couldn't fly over when you asked him. Or that delightful Seamus Lochlann." Shanley smiled.

"Yeah. Um." Ceri sucked in air. "Turns out, Rio is my warrior."

Shanley staggered into the chair beside her front door. "Get out. Rio Sheridan? How did you not know this before you flew over to Conlan Manor? You two met when? Last winter?"

"It's a long story, but the abbreviated version is I need you to come over here. Hamish says we have to complete an important ritual on Samhain—one that involves you. I know it's short notice, but—"

"I'll figure something out." Shanley stared at the piles of snow outside the window of her townhouse. "You don't sound too happy about this most fortunate turn of events."

"Rio never made it a secret he didn't like me. Turns out he had some good reasons… in his mind."

"Things you can fix, right?"

Ceri's tone held an edge. "I'm not a flirt, Shanley, something he needs to understand."

"*What?* Is he handy? I'd like to give him a piece of my mind."

Ceri laughed weakly. "You'll have your chance when you come to Scotland."

"There's something else. Out with it."

"It seems prophecies follow the Sheridan family—and apparently ours. Anyway, we need to complete this ritual to continue righting the wrongs the evil trio initiated a millennium ago. Aunt Shanley, I'm scared."

It'd been a long time since Ceri had addressed her as "Aunt," which told Shanley there was no choice about joining her niece in Scotland at Samhain.

"I'll be there. You have Hamish. And now Rio. It'll work out."

"Promise?"

"Oh, sweetheart. You know there are no guarantees. But there's training and planning and the occasionally terrifying machinations of a determined old druid. Everything is going to be fine."

"Thank you. I know that. I think I just needed to hear you say it."

Shanley smiled. "I have to go or I'll be late for work." Deliberately changing her tone, she said, "I know the two of you need to bond, so I won't be upset if I don't reach you later. I'll keep trying until you're free to talk again."

Ceri made a noncommittal sound.

"I'm so glad you've found your warrior. You two will work out your issues, I'm sure. That's what bonding is for. Plus, you'll be busy figuring out your complementary skill to aid him in battle." Shanley shouldered her purse. "You're safe with Hamish in Conlan Manor. Talk to you soon."

After she hung up, she stared unseeingly at her phone for several minutes. If tall, dark-haired, blue-eyed Rio Sheridan was Ceri's warrior, who was the burly auburn-haired man haunting Shanley's mind?

⁓

"You're going where?" Logan asked as he followed Shanley around her small kitchen, looming over her as she put the finishing touches on their dinner.

At last, she spun around and stomped her foot. "Logan Malo, if you don't stop stalking me, we're never going to eat." She tried to soften her tone by tapping her date lightly on the chest with the wooden spoon she'd grabbed to stir the spaghetti sauce bubbling gently on her stove.

Logan sighed a bit overdramatically for her taste and retreated to the table where he sat down heavily and took a long pull from the beer he'd grabbed from the fridge. *Civilian men can be such divas* flitted through her mind as she watched him.

"Like I told you, my niece inherited a manor house in Scotland, and she's throwing a big party for Halloween—a party she wants me to attend. I can't very well pass up such a great opportunity. I haven't been over there since I graduated from college," she said over her shoulder as she ladled sauce into a serving dish.

"But I thought we had plans for Halloween. I told you when we met that it was my favorite holiday." The pout on his lips didn't enhance his pretty face.

"I'm sorry, Logan. But Ceri moved over there recently, and I think she's homesick."

Logan rolled his eyes as she set the food on the table, and it was all she could do not to roll hers back at him. When he'd burst into her life a few weeks ago on his first day of substitute teaching, she'd thought him charming in a boyish way. But the more she got to know him, the more she detected a certain cruelty to the features his pretty boy vibe disguised. *About the only thing he has in common with the auburn-haired warrior is the breadth of his shoulders and the thickness of his chest.*

Shanley blinked. *Where did that come from?*

"How are you getting the time off? Isn't it the middle of the term?" Logan asked as he dished about half the food on the table onto his plate.

She helped herself to a reasonable portion of pasta and spread a ladleful of sauce over it. "I have personal leave saved. It's no big deal." A thought occurred to her. "Maybe you can cover my classes while I'm gone. You know so much about history, you'd be an ace at taking over for me."

"I might be busy then too." He shoveled food into his mouth and didn't look at her.

"Look, Logan. I'm sorry I can't go out with you on Halloween. But it's not like I'm moving over to Scotland to live with my niece."

He grunted.

"Tell you what. When I get back, we'll throw a costume party." She sipped her glass of merlot, warming to the idea. "Maybe something with a historical theme."

"Yeah, whatever."

Shanley sighed. She'd only started dating Logan Malo a couple weeks ago, but it appeared he was like most of the other civilians she'd dated in the past. Moody, self-absorbed, a little bit spoiled. Definitely not a long-term prospect. Not for the first time, she wondered what type of man the gods had chosen for her warrior. Because obviously, left to her own devices, she was a lousy judge of men.

CHAPTER SEVEN

DINNER FOLLOWING RIO Sheridan's discovery of Ceri Ross as his talisman had been an altogether pleasant affair, Alaisdair thought. Much more enjoyable than previous meals he'd shared with a suspicious and openly hostile Rio.

Of course, he couldn't blame the man once Rio discovered Alaisdair had tried his sign on Ceri and had discovered her visualization weaknesses. Holding himself back from a woman he desperately wanted but thought would cause his downfall—and eventual death—must have taken an incredible toll on Rio's peace of mind.

Alaisdair could sympathize.

Even so, Alaisdair had liked the man from the first time they'd met. After sparring with Rio in the training room at *An Teallach*, his respect for the younger warrior's incredible skills cemented Alaisdair's good opinion. The only fly in the ointment had been Rio's inexplicable attitude toward the mistress of the manor— an attitude he'd only partially justified, to Alaisdair's way of thinking.

After dinner, Rio and Ceri excused themselves to their private quarters, something expected of a newly mated warrior and talisman pair. As much as Ceri seemed embarrassed about it, none of the men thought a thing untoward. Bonding was necessary, and fortunately, quite enjoyable. Not that Alaisdair knew from personal experience.

With Rio safely out of earshot, Hamish said, "The twa o' them was meant tae be taegether. Every time I see 'em, it becomes clearer. But I'm still sorry she wasnae the one fer ye, auld friend."

Not having discovered his talisman before midnight of his twenty-eighth birthday nearly fourteen years ago, Alaisdair had gone into hiding at Conlan Manor. Being a distant relation to the Conlan clan, he'd been able to enjoy the protections Hamish offered as long as he never left the grounds of their ancestral home. As prisons went, he knew he could do much worse. Then again, imprisonment at Conlan Manor was a far superior fate to the alternatives—death or life on the run or dishonor as a rogue warrior serving the bloodthirsty whims of an angry trio of war goddesses who deemed him expendable—especially when one or the other of them wanted an orgasm.

"I am tae. She's a stunning woman." Alaisdair stared at the staircase where Rio had led Ceri up to the master suite. Shaking himself, he gathered dishes and walked them over to the sink. "Why donnae ye grab yer gear and be on yer way? I'll take care of the washin' up. Better ye reach the city before full dark."

"Thank ye, Alaisdair."

Hamish disappeared down the hallway off the kitchen only to reappear a minute later carrying a small knapsack. "One other thin' ye need tae know," he said as he walked to the back door. "The whole Sheridan clan is comin' in sometime taemorrow. Rio's father telephoned. They're bringin' along more security equipment, so they're rentin' cars and drivin' themselves up tae Ullapool from Inverness."

Alaisdair shook his head and grinned. "Even after they learned I'm Ceri's prowler, they're still plannin' tae wire up the manor with their high-tech equipment?"

"Seems tae be the way o' it. Ye might stay near the phone in case they need directions—and Rio is otherwise occupied." Hamish chortled.

"Ye dinnae tell Ceri and Rio about his family's arrival? Why?"

"If they're busy bondin' when the family arrives, all the better. Then there's nae doubt among them that she belongs tae their clan as well."

Wiping his wet hands on a towel, Alaisdair furrowed his brow. "I had the impression they all knew and liked each other already." He leaned against the sink and stared at Hamish.

"Yeah, I believe that tae be true, but it never hurts tae add layers." Hamish winked.

"I should have known that's how ye'd look at it, auld man." Alaisdair laughed. "I'll be waitin' fer them. Are there any unattached talismans in their clan by chance?" he asked hopefully.

"As far as I know, the clan runs tae sons. Perhaps ye'll meet yer talisman at the ceilidh on Samhain."

"Even with the reprieve the Sheridans created fer warriors last winter, time's runnin' out fer me, Hamish."

"All will be well, Alaisdair. Have faith."

On that parting note, Hamish walked out into the still afternoon while Alaisdair finished cleaning up lunch.

What he honestly wanted to do was spend time in the manor library, his usual occupation of an afternoon. But with Ceri and Rio bonding a few steps down the hall, he thought he'd be intruding. Instead, he headed to the sitting room beside the front entrance to the manor to watch some lame afternoon telly while he awaited the Sheridans' arrival.

⁊

After landing in Inverness, Shanley headed for baggage claim where she found Hamish on the balls of his feet, bouncing up and down like a kid at Christmas. Something about the gnomish old man dancing in happy anticipation of her arrival reached inside her and tickled her as well. She was laughing when they met in a warm embrace.

"I take it you missed me, Hamish."

"I did indeed, lass. I did indeed. It's been far tae long."

Holding her hands in his, he stepped back from her and took her in from head to toe. "Ye havnae changed a bit, Shanley. Still as bonny as ever."

"Neither have you, you old charmer." She grinned.

Looking past her shoulder, he asked, "Who is this with ye?"

"This is Finn Daly. Finn, meet Hamish Buchanan, the druid I told you about."

As the two men shook hands, Shanley said, "Finn lost his talisman years ago and took on protecting Ceri and me as well as Ceri's friend Alyssa and Alyssa's druid grandmother." She quirked a brow. "Afton Sinclair could rival your prowess as a druid, I think."

"I'd like tae meet her," Hamish said.

"Sadly, we lost Afton over a year ago," Finn said, his dear smile turned upside down.

"Thank ye fer coming. We're happy tae have ye join us, Finn. Shanley told me she wouldnae made the trip without yer protection."

Finn nodded. "I've always wanted to see Scotland."

"Let's gather up yer bags and head home before Ceri does somethin' alarmin' and tries tae visualize herself here tae greet ye."

Shanley looked around the baggage claim area. "She's not here?"

The twinkle left Hamish's eye. "It's tae dangerous, lass. She's precious, that one. Until we finish the ritual at Samhain, we

donnae want her anywhere except the manor and the trainin'
room at *An Teallach*. Scathach gave orders about that."

She raised a brow. "Scathach is here?"

"Which one o' these bags is yers, lass?"

She stepped over to the carousel, her timing perfect as she
reached for the tartan-patterned suitcase she'd packed.

"Got it," Hamish said as he reached past her and grabbed the
handle of her bag.

Finn pulled his suitcase from the carousel while Shanley
shouldered her oversized purse-cum-carry-on bag. Hamish led
the way through the airport and out into a perfect autumn day,
the crisp atmosphere intensifying the blue of the sky. Stopping
for a moment, she sucked in a lungful of clean Scots air before
she hustled to catch up to Hamish and Finn.

"At least ye dinnae pack fer the winter," he said as he dropped
her case into the space behind the back seat of his MINI Cooper
before he came around to open her door. "I thought I might have
tae strap some o' Ceri's luggage tae the roof tae drive her tae the
manor." They smiled together with understanding. Finn waited
until Hamish closed the door before he opened the back compartment and slid into the seat behind Shanley.

"You've upgraded your ride, I see. Very nice," she said as she
belted herself in. "Now what's this about Scathach?"

"No' goin' tae let that one go, eh lass?"

"Nope."

Hamish turned the ignition of the little car, put it in gear,
and drove out of the airport on a roundabout route she knew
would have them skirting the city. As much as she wished to take
a detour through Inverness, the beautiful capital of the Highlands,
she wanted to see Conlan Manor and Ceri even more.

"Seems the Sheridans are particular favorites o' the auld girl,
and she trains 'em and their talismans personally. She works Rio
especially hard, but after watchin' the lad train, I understand her

interest. That boy is nearly godlike in his battle prowess." Hamish slid her a side-long glance. "A mite terrifyin' actually."

"I can confirm both observations," Finn said with a laugh. "I trained with Rio and Scathach at the Sheridan compound last winter before Morgan made off with Alyssa. Rio is a formidable warrior."

Shanley stared incredulously at Hamish. "You were baiting him, why again?"

"When the lad stepped over the threshold o' Conlan Manor, I felt a ripple in the cosmos that raised all my hair."

She chuckled, envisioning the picture of *Back to the Future*'s Doc Brown his description brought to mind before she sobered. "You knew he was her warrior?"

"Nae. Ye know Danu and the Dagda keep that particular information tae themselves. But I sensed he was someone special tae the manor. I wanted tae keep him around." Hamish waited his turn in the roundabout on the western edge of the city before joining traffic to cross the Firth of Moray via the Kessock Bridge. "Baitin' him was entertainin'—"

Shanley glared at him.

He shrugged. "And it served the purpose o' learnin' about the lad. Fer instance, he doesnae think tae highly o' druids. We're goin' tae have tae help him with that."

"I'm sure you've already been working on it," she said dryly and sat back to enjoy the scenery as they traveled beside the slate-blue waters of the firth before turning west toward Ullapool.

Birch forests in glorious autumnal yellows and oranges gave way to the long chartreuse grasses disguising the dark volcanic slate of the hillsides the farther west they traveled. When they crested the hill outside of Ullapool, Loch Broom sparkled in the late afternoon sunshine. Turning north, they followed the winding road leading them to the manor. At the top of the long drive, Hamish stopped the car, giving Shanley and Finn the chance to enjoy the golden glow of Conlan Manor as its sandstone façade reflected the setting sun.

Like the first time she saw it, this view of the manor stole her breath. The evergreens of the formal front gardens were perfectly arranged and trimmed to form a series of Celtic trinity knots, which she knew sheltered various herbs and flowers Hamish liked to use in his potions, salves, and meals. Even from this distance, she could see some of the late season flowers blooming purple and pink against their dark green backdrops.

The water in the central fountain danced even this late in the year, catching sunbeams like cascading diamonds before dropping back into the basin beneath it. A profusion of late-blooming yellow chrysanthemums, purple asters, and bright lavender primroses threatened to fall out of the planters arranged around the fountain. Tears brimmed in her eyes as she tried to internalize the view. If she lived to be ninety, she knew she'd never tire of seeing the splendor of Conlan Manor during an autumn sunset.

Finn blew out a breath. "This is some place Ceri inherited."

"It definitely is," Shanley whispered over the lump in her throat.

Hamish made a satisfied sound and put the car back in gear, driving around to the carpark situated at the back of the manor so as not to obstruct that magnificent view.

"In the auld days," Hamish explained to Finn, "the view of the manor from the hilltop served as a warning tae enemies and a reassurance tae friends that the house was strong and protected."

"It's certainly an impressive sight," Finn said.

Based on what little Hamish and Ceri had told her so far, Shanley hoped for the truth of the house's strength still.

CHAPTER EIGHT

"LAYERS, LASS, LAYERS. Ye should know that about Hamish by now," Alaisdair said as he descended the last step into the kitchen, Ceri on his heels. "Hello Hamish. Successful trip, I trust?"

"We have the reinforcements we'll need fer Samhain. All is in place."

Alaisdair nodded before turning back to Ceri who looked thoroughly confused.

Then she returned to her wailing theme. "Hamish, couldn't you have at least given us a heads-up that Rio's family was coming in this afternoon?"

Alaisdair grinned at Ceri before she drew his attention to the stunning woman who stepped out from behind Hamish.

"Shanley! You made it! I'm so happy to see you," she gushed as she threw herself into the arms of the most beautiful woman Alaisdair had ever seen.

He watched dumbfounded as the woman, Shanley, said, "Ceri, *I'm* so happy to see *you*."

She pulled back and gave Ceri a long once-over.

"Conlan Manor agrees with you, sweetie. Either that or bonding with your warrior. I can't decide," she teased.

Alaisdair couldn't stop staring. *Beautiful and a sense of humor? Now I'm in trouble.*

"You too?" Ceri cried. "I thought of all people, you wouldn't draw attention to that."

"Why would you think that?" Shanley asked with a sly grin in Hamish's direction. "After all, I think I was the one tasked with educating you about what to expect."

Ceri's tone took on a decided sadness. "You have no idea what it's like, Shanley. I'm truly sorry about that."

Alaisdair wrinkled his brow. *What does Ceri mean by that?*

Shanley pulled Ceri into another embrace, smoothing her hand over Ceri's hair, a lighter shade of her own without the red highlights. "We've been over it a thousand times. Some of us never find our fated mates. It seems unjust, I know, but it's the way it is. I accepted it long ago. You need to do the same."

A man standing near Hamish cleared his throat, drawing Alaisdair's attention away from the two women.

"Hello, Ceri," he said, stepping forward. "Scotland agrees with you. You look beautiful."

"Finn! Thank you! If not for you, I doubt Shanley would have made the trip." Ceri wrapped her arms around an old warrior and squeezed.

Alaisdair couldn't stand it. "These folks are obviously important tae ye, Ceri. Introductions?"

"Sorry," she said, glancing sheepishly at him. "Alaisdair, this is my aunt, Shanley Conlan." She turned to her stunning aunt. "Shanley. This is Alaisdair Graham, a warrior who helps Hamish look after the manor. And this is our old friend, Finn Daly."

Shanley stood stone-still and stared at him, while the old warrior, Finn, stepped up to him and clasped his elbow in the age-old way warriors greeted each other. "A pleasure," Finn said, giving him an assessing look. No mistaking the challenge there.

Alaisdair nodded politely to Finn, but his attention remained on Shanley.

She blinked at him for several seconds before she swallowed, visibly recovering herself. "Pleased to meet you, Alaisdair," she said, extending a hand to him.

He cleared his throat. "Likewise. It's apparent ye're related tae Ceri. The resemblance is remarkable." His eyes saucered as electricity tingled up his arm from where his hand held Shanley's. Looking into her face, he watched her eyes widen at the touch of their hands.

The world fell away as Alaisdair lost himself in her eyes. If he could have, he would have taken a walk in the mysterious forests of Shanley's eyes. The tiny crow's feet bracketing those eyes told him Shanley Conlan loved to laugh. Her straight nose guided his gaze to her full lips. Lips he longed to taste while he buried his hands in the strawberry-blond mass of hair falling over her shoulders.

He rubbed his thumb over the soft skin of her hand, and the tingling sensation grew stronger. His heart hammered in his chest at the weight of her hand in his. All he wanted to do was spirit this woman away to his cottage and forget everything but her.

Hamish's booming voice broke the spell.

"Are the Sheridans upstairs? We should go on up and join 'em. Have ye shown 'em the house yet?" Hamish asked as if nothing in the world was happening between Alaisdair and Shanley.

Reluctantly, Alaisdair let Shanley go. Was it his imagination, or was she reluctant to let him go too?

"N-no," Ceri answered. Her eyes imitated a tennis match as she looked from her aunt to Alaisdair and back again.

"We should get tae it then, settle 'em intae their rooms and such. Come on Alaisdair, Shanley, Finn. Let's go take care o' our guests," a jovial Hamish said as he headed for the stairs.

As he neared her, Hamish drew Ceri's hand into the crook of his arm to lead the way, and Finn stepped in behind them. Shanley gave Alaisdair one last shell-shocked glance before she followed the others.

Alaisdair stood alone in the middle of the kitchen, hands on hips, and stared unseeing at the ceiling. *If this woman isnae my talisman, I'm in serious trouble.*

Blowing out a breath and rolling his shoulders, he shook those thoughts from his head. Taking the stairs two at a time, he entered the grand salon seconds behind the Conlans.

For several hours, Ceri and Rio led the Sheridan family around the manor, showing them the house from bottom to top. Shanley followed the crowd and reabsorbed the house she'd loved as a young woman with big dreams of her warrior finding her. She'd dreamed they would share a life devoted to each other and to saving civilians, other warriors, and druids from the evil machinations of the trio of vengeful goddesses who had an eternity to fill with their quest for sexual pleasure at mortals' expense.

Not having found her warrior had dashed those fantasies years ago. Then she'd looked up from hugging Ceri hello and saw the man who had haunted her premonitions for over a decade standing in the middle of the ancient kitchen of Conlan Manor. As she half listened to Rio and Ceri explain the security system they were installing in the manor, her reaction to Alaisdair Graham troubled her. How could she respond as she had to a warrior well past his twenty-eighth birthday? At his touch, her breath had backed up in her throat. Her whole body arced with electricity bolting to her center and leaving a delicious heaviness low in her belly. But this warrior had to belong to another talisman. No way could he have escaped the notice—and the wrath and greed of the unholy trio long enough to grow the graying strands she'd noticed burnishing the glorious auburn of his tied-back shoulder-length hair.

He'd held her hand long past polite, a fact that bothered her even more than her reaction to him. Several times as the group walked through the house, she'd caught him staring at her. His whisky-colored eyes burned into hers every time their eyes met. Having the entire Sheridan family along, not just Ceri's best friend Alyssa and her husband, Rowan, but also Rio's parents Owen and Sian, and his twin brother and sister-in-law Riley and Lynnette, made it easy for Shanley to keep her physical distance from Alaisdair Graham. Too bad she found herself struggling to keep her mental and emotional distance.

Why couldn't she keep her thoughts and attention on reacquainting herself with the manor? Even though the house remained basically the same as when she'd last seen it years ago, there were subtle changes. The carpets on the stairwells had been upgraded from the faded brown she remembered to a deep mauve. Fresh paint on the walls enlivened the portraits lining the halls. And someone had given the ballroom a deep clean recently and changed the drapes. The lavender, green, and heather hues of the Conlan tartan drapes on the windows almost glowed off the opposite walls and the gleaming hardwood floor.

Yet again, her gaze strayed from the house, and her focus strayed from Ceri's and Rio's conversation to Alaisdair Graham who stood near the back of the assembled Sheridans. His massive arms folded over his equally impressive chest in the long-sleeved tan Henley he wore. As she'd stood behind him a couple of times during the afternoon, she'd tamped down her lady-parts' reactions to the sight of his long lean legs and tight backside encased in easy-fit jeans. His thick hair pulled back in a neat ponytail curled naturally. Though a couple of inches shorter than the Sheridans who each topped six feet, he lacked nothing in stature.

However attractive his whole package, though, the intensity of those whisky-colored eyes dragged her to him repeatedly. For all her attempts to keep her attention where it should be, she couldn't prevent herself from returning his stare over and over again. For his part, he didn't seem to care about anything or anyone but her. Which proved he either had no scruples or he had no clue about the family into which Ceri was now bonded.

She puffed out a disgusted breath at herself and deliberately turned her attention to the fireplace at the front of the room. As her gaze wandered over the massive painting of a long-ago battle in which the Conlan clan fought valiantly, her thoughts wandered back in time too. The tales of talismans who didn't remain true to their warriors and the warriors who pursued other men's talismans littered the histories of the great heroes. Civilians liked to think of those stories as myths and legends, but as a historian not only in the civilian world but also in the warrior realm, Shanley knew the truth.

Tristan and Isolde came to mind. They died because not one, but two unscrupulous warriors coveted Isolde and denied her true warrior to live with her after they bonded. Their circumstances didn't stop the two of them from meeting clandestinely and renewing their love and commitment to each other, but they were never the united team the fates destined them to be. In the end, the goddesses collected all the players in that little tragedy because King Mark waited too long to give Isolde up, and Andred practiced treachery, no doubt egged on by the likes of Morgan or Maeve. When Isolde watched Tristan's blood swirling in the ford as he passed over with Morgan into the afterlife, she gave herself up to The White Lady and crossed into the mists. King Mark and Andred suffered their deserved fates and fed Morgan's bloodlust soon after.

Tristan and Isolde's story stood as an object lesson for other warriors. The thought of giving herself to a rogue warrior, no matter how handsome, no matter how compelling, roiled Shanley's stomach. The kind of divine treachery necessary to have her watching scenes about the man in her mind all these years compounded her misery. She'd give herself up to The White Lady rather than live in disrepute as the talisman mistress of a rogue warrior.

Finn's low voice at her elbow pulled her from her morbid thoughts. "You're looking a little green, Shanley. Do you need to lie down? I think that flight took a lot out of you."

She flinched and cleared her throat to recover herself. "Sorry you had to see that, Finn. I've always been a lousy flier. Airsick every time." She gave him a self-deprecating smile. "I think I'll sit for a minute."

The group had toured the house from the kitchens in the basement to the massive ballroom on the third story. She sat in one of the straight-backed chairs lining the room, the plush padding of its tartan-covered seat welcome. In the background, Rio was saying something about securing the floor-to-ceiling windows looking out over the front gardens.

"I'm a bit worn out myself." Finn patted her knee in a grandfatherly way as he took a seat beside her.

Having taken the chair nearest the double door into the room, she was grateful Finn sat beside her, thereby blocking any ideas Alaisdair might have of joining her. Perhaps it crossed his mind too as he cocked a brow first in her direction then in Finn's when he caught her eye yet again.

"This is the whole house?" Rowan asked, interrupting Alaisdair and Shanley's silent conversation.

"Except for the attic and the roof," Rio replied. "Unfortunately, the roof is accessible from that window-looking door in the corner by the fireplace. Via a treacherous exterior staircase."

The glare he turned on Hamish confused Shanley. Why would Rio be upset about the fire escape?

"We explained all that," Hamish said amiably. "Yer girl is safe and sound and no' the worse fer wear. She needed tae chant the rituals over the entire manor, Rio. No' negotiable."

Rio snorted in disgust while Ceri stared helplessly between the two. Whatever the problem, Shanley thought she could help.

"My sister, Becca, walked the manor—all of it—when Ceri was still a toddler. A year later, I chanted over it. If you don't look down, those stairs aren't a big deal."

"*What?* All the women in this family have been on that death-trap?" Rio asked, taking a menacing step in Hamish's direction.

"This is the family seat, Rio. The women in the family own—and protect it. Which makes having them chant over it necessary." Hamish's usual jovial tone had vanished.

Apparently, this was an ongoing argument.

"Our women are the lifeblood o' this house. Dae ye truly think I'd let any harm come tae them?"

A charged silence ensued as Rio glared at Hamish. In Shanley's admittedly limited acquaintance with the man, she'd observed Rio was a warrior through and through. After what Finn had revealed about Scathach's interest in him, no doubt he was something special in the warrior community. But in the end, Rio sucked in a breath, stepped over to Ceri to slide his arm around her, and deferred to Hamish.

Shanley watched in fascination as Ceri blinked up at her warrior before shyly sliding an arm around him too. Turning her attention to the assembled family, she said, "Now that you've seen the manor, it's time to settle everyone into their rooms. We've prepared rooms on the second floor for you—"

Finn interrupted. "If it's all the same to you, Ceri, I'd like one of the smaller rooms down the hall from this one. I don't require much space."

"Are you sure, Finn? There are plenty of rooms on the second floor."

Finn waved a hand. "Bah. With all your coming and going and noise, how will I ever sleep?"

Shanley turned her head and furrowed her brow at him until she saw the twinkle in his eye.

"I've lived on my own for so long that I like my solitude. Just make sure you have a place set for me at dinner."

"Seems a perfect idea tae me," Hamish added. "The twa auld ones guarding the house from top tae bottom."

"When you put it that way—" Ceri began.

Hamish winked at Finn who winked back. The two of them being on the same page so quickly after their initial meeting didn't surprise Shanley. She'd known both of them a long time.

Throughout the entire exchange, Alaisdair Graham stood apart from the rest of the party, but his attention never strayed from her. Between the argument that didn't reach its boiling point but still simmered quietly, her jet lag, and her disquieting response to a warrior of questionable background and intentions, Shanley welcomed some time to herself. Rising from her seat, she patted Finn on the shoulder and turned toward the door.

"I'll take the room immediately to the left at the top of the stairs," she announced before looking back at the Sheridans. "I realize it's selfish of me to take one of the best rooms overlooking the gardens, but that's where I stayed when I spent my year here, and I'm comfortable there."

Ceri disengaged herself from Rio's side and walked over to Shanley. "Hamish told me that, so I had the room made up for you. No worries." She reached out and squeezed Shanley's hand. "When you've freshened up, we'll all meet downstairs for dinner. Hamish has something delicious cooking."

"Dinner, you said?" Finn asked, standing between Shanley and Ceri to hug both of them to his sides. "I'm all for that. Let's get ourselves situated so we can eat."

CHAPTER NINE

T FINN'S PRONOUNCEMENT, the brewing tension blew out of the ballroom like letting air out of a balloon. Everyone trooped back down the stairs, through the main entryway, down to the kitchens, and out to the carpark to retrieve luggage. In all the confusion, Alaisdair easily grabbed Shanley's suitcase and pretended not to hear her when she said she could take care of it herself. At least he waited outside her bedroom door for an invitation before he carried it into her room.

Jasmine and musk wafted over him as she slipped past him through the doorway. She deposited her huge purse on the antique bureau that stood on the right of the tiny en suite bathroom's doorway. Turning to Alaisdair who remained right inside the door, she said, "You can drop that in front of the wardrobe, thanks. I've got it from here."

"This is it, lass?" He hefted her suitcase that seemed to be filled with nothing but air. "One piece o' luggage and that oversized bag? Dae ye always travel so light?"

"I won't be staying long. Only through Samhain. Even with whatever magic Hamish practiced long-distance on my boss"—her mischievous smile said there was a story there—"I still have a job to go home to."

"What is it that ye dae, if ye donnae mind my askin'?"

She crossed her arms over her thick lavender-colored sweater that didn't tell him nearly enough about her and yet told him plenty. For some reason, she wanted to avoid him, which made him want to know even more about her aside from the fact she was an unattached talisman. That much of the conversation she'd had with Ceri minutes after her arrival was branded on his brain.

"I teach history in a high school in Montana."

He smiled. "Nae wonder ye were so reluctant tae leave the library earlier."

At her gasp, he dropped her case at the door. In two strides, he stood in front of her. "What is it lass? Are ye all right?"

She took a step back. In the nick of time, he stopped his hands from closing in on her upper arms, their decided destination.

"When you—" She waved a hand in front of her face. "Oh Lord." Closing her eyes, she tried to compose herself. "Never mind."

The rosy color staining her cheekbones rendered her even more lovely in his eyes. He'd had little opportunity to spend time with beautiful women over the last twelve or thirteen years, so he didn't want to chance blowing it by drawing attention to her blush. Stuffing down the teasing remark on the tip of his tongue, he said, "The library is my favorite room in the manor tae."

Fascinated, he watched her embarrassment morph into suspicion in a nanosecond.

"What do you do, Alaisdair Graham, that allows you to spend so much time here? I don't remember seeing you around when I spent my year in this house."

Giving her space, he walked over to the window and looked out at the gardens. "I help Hamish take care of the place. It's quite a pile o' rocks fer one man tae look after, even one as ingenious as that auld druid," he said with a chuckle.

"You live here?"

At the accusation in her tone, he crossed his arms over his chest and faced her.

"I live in the cottage at the edge o' the manor's lands tae the north."

"Will your talisman be joining us later?"

He'd known the question would come at some time or other. After all, the anomaly of him avoiding Morgan, Maeve, and Macha all these years would most definitely merit it. Yet for some reason, it grated on him coming from a woman to whom he was so attracted—a talisman whose warrior had never found her.

"I donnae have a talisman."

"I see," she said, her whole demeanor telling him she most definitely did not see. "Thanks for carrying my luggage up here. If you don't mind, I'd like to settle in now."

He stared at her for one long beat before he nodded and walked over to the door. Without a word, he picked up her suitcase from where he'd dropped it earlier and placed on the floor in front of the freestanding wardrobe that served as a closet for the room. Turning on his heel, he walked out, tugging the door closed behind him.

In the hallway outside Shanley's door, he blew a frustrated breath at the ceiling. The woman obviously pegged him as a rogue at best, a coward at worst. And it wasn't a given she even belonged to him. Just because she was an unattached talisman of a certain age didn't mean he was her warrior. Just because his desperation to find his talisman colored the few encounters he'd had with women over the last fourteen years didn't mean he could make any assumptions about her. Just because he found her so damn beautiful didn't mean she'd welcome him now even if she was his talisman. Going to ground for all these years came with a steep price.

Hamish's happy whistling greeted Alaisdair on the stairs as he descended them into the kitchen. At least he knew Hamish would always be glad to see him.

"Ye're soundin' rather pleased with yerself. What have ye done this time auld man?"

"Och, Alaisdair. Always assumin' there's an angle," Hamish said with a wink.

Aye, there was an angle. "Who's in yer crosshairs this time?" Alaisdair asked as he automatically stepped in to chop the vegetables Hamish had laid out for a salad.

Hamish chuckled as he pulled a massive pan of shepherd's pie from the oven and set it on the table. Alaisdair dropped the knife he'd been wielding and grabbed another pair of hot pads to retrieve the second pie from the oven, placing it on the table beside the first.

"Warrior blood runs deep in these Sheridans. I imagine our Samhain celebration will include all sorts o' fireworks this year, even more than I anticipated when it was only Rio Sheridan invited tae the party."

Hamish pulled a pan of apple cobbler from the refrigerator and placed it in the still-warm oven. Then he joined Alaisdair who'd resumed his salad preparations. "The whole bunch is virile and passionate. I'm quite pleased tae have them related tae us."

"And ye've made some adjustments tae yer usual recipes tae ensure that passion benefits Conlan Manor." Alaisdair shook his head and didn't bother to hide the grin playing over his mouth.

"Have I taught ye naethin', lad? It never hurts tae—"

"—add layers," Alaisdair finished for him with a chuckle.

"Exactly. Now if ye'll carry that salad tae the dining room, I'll call the clan tae dinner."

Alaisdair hoped whatever Hamish had planned included some

help for him finding his talisman. He understood the peril the latest Samhain celebration posed, one even more dangerous than those he'd avoided every single year since he'd turned twenty-eight alone. By some ancient agreement between the manor's matriarch Fianna Conlan and the deities of the Celtic pantheon, Hamish always invited the gods. Specifically, the Morrigan since it was her feast day. Staying out of her sights all these years had been especially difficult during this time of year.

He understood the precariousness of his situation in the manor. With the wrath the Sheridans stirred up in Morgan last year, he had no doubt she'd rain down her revenge when the battle Hamish anticipated erupted on Samhain. Which put him at even greater risk without a talisman's help.

As he placed the salad at the end of the long dining room table closest to the doorway and pulled plates and utensils from the sideboard to set the table, he thought about Shanley Conlan. Though the woman was justifiably wary of him, he couldn't ignore the currents of awareness that swirled between them. Maybe it was their unattached status. Maybe it was something else.

A quiet knock sounded at her door as Shanley reacquainted herself with her "old" room.

"It's open."

She looked up from filling a bureau drawer with her underwear to catch Ceri popping her head inside the room.

"Are you settling in okay?"

Shanley smiled. "It's like coming home almost. Isn't that weird?"

Ceri laughed. "Yeah, it is, especially since you haven't even eaten yet."

Shanley furrowed her brow before she remembered. "He's been working on you too, has he? It's a good thing there are so few rogue druids. With the subtle ways they can exert power, we'd always be in danger if they weren't predisposed to be healers and helpers," she said with a grin before she sobered. "Shouldn't you be with Rio?"

Ceri squeezed her eyes shut before she stepped fully into the room and closed the door behind her.

"We were right in the middle of things when an unholy racket sounded at the front door not long before you arrived. Shanley, Sian Sheridan nearly walked in on us."

Shanley struggled to stifle a giggle as Ceri sat down hard on the chair beside the door and dropped her head into her hands.

Smoothing a hand over her distraught niece's shoulder, she said, "I take it you didn't know they were arriving today."

"No. Apparently, Hamish 'forgot' to mention it. I've never been so mortified in all my life," she huffed. "Some first impression I made on my warrior's family." She slumped against the back of the chair and stared balefully up at Shanley.

"That was probably the best first impression you could have made, under the circumstances. After all, if you two were a pair who doesn't bond, they might be less excited about being here with you. Especially with Hamish's ominous predictions for Samhain."

"One would have thought Alaisdair at least would have said something," Ceri complained.

Shanley froze.

"What do you mean by that?"

"He's the one who let them in like he was expecting them or something."

Shanley wandered over to the bed and sank down on it. "Tell me about him. Why is a rogue warrior living under the protections of Conlan Manor?"

Ceri's eyes rounded. "He's not a rogue, Shanley. Alaisdair Graham went to ground when he didn't find his talisman in time. He's related to the Conlans, so Hamish took him in and keeps him safe on the manor grounds. In return, Alaisdair watches out for the manor."

"So." She blew out a breath. "He's a coward."

Ceri slanted her a look before she stood and walked over to the windows to gaze out at the impressive front gardens. Shanley understood their allure. It's why she chose the room she did. But that didn't answer the question.

"He's honorable and brave." Ceri's voice resonated with passionate defense. "He came upon me out on the grounds one day, and I thought I faced your fate when you were here." Facing Shanley, she lifted an expressive brow before returning her attention to the gardens beyond the windows. "Hamish had driven Rio to the training room, so I was on my own. I tried to visualize myself out of the situation, but Alaisdair stopped me because of who he is and what he knew of my plans as soon as I made them."

"What do you mean?"

Ceri seemed not to have heard her. "Of course, once he discovered my warrior had found me, he thought it his duty to tell Rio about my weakness, and Hamish declared we'd set it to rights immediately, so we started training yesterday."

"What weakness?"

"I can't shield my thoughts well when I'm facing imminent danger."

Shanley sighed. "I'm sorry, Ceri. Without access to a training room, I couldn't set actual traps for you to work your way out of." Rubbing her hands down her thighs, she added, "I'd hoped with your intelligence, you'd managed to build a strong shield. You certainly can keep me out of your head when you want to."

Ceri crossed her arms over her chest and continued to stare out the window. "I know," she said quietly. "It's not your fault. Besides, my lack of a strong shield gave Scathach her excuse to push my training to another level."

"Is that when you discovered your skill?"

Ceri turned wide eyes on her, and Shanley shrugged.

"I noticed the change in you as you and Rio showed us the house this afternoon. It's obvious your bonding has progressed rather rapidly."

"I had a vision about Rio, and"—she swallowed—"and it was terrifying." Ceri walked over and slumped down on the bed beside Shanley. "Scathach thinks it's 'wonderful' that my skill is prophecy." Ceri glanced up at the ceiling. "But I don't know how I'm going to take watching Rio die over and over again even in visions."

Shanley rubbed Ceri's back. "If that's your skill, you must embrace it. Now that you know you're not actually seeing Rio die, having the visions will become easier," she said quietly.

The sorrow in Ceri's voice nearly undid her.

"I don't know, Shanley. Over the last weeks as we worked together to put in the security system, I developed feelings for him, even when I didn't know he was my warrior. Which was terrifying." She sighed. "Now that we've discovered he's my mate, the thought of losing him tears me up."

Shanley hugged Ceri close and whispered into her hair, "None of us has a guarantee. Not even with our heightened skills and abilities. At our core, we're all mortal. We all face risk. Our advantage is we can mitigate that risk when we work together with our destined partner." She pushed Ceri's hair over her shoulder. "You're a prophetess."

Ceri nodded.

"That's a tremendous advantage. You have the ability to help Rio change what will happen because you can see what *might* happen. If you look at your special skill that way, perhaps it will be easier to bear."

"Now you sound like Scathach."

The grumpiness in Ceri's tone heartened Shanley.

"I like that. Being compared to the warrior goddess is right up my alley." She grinned.

Ceri rolled her eyes just as Hamish interrupted over the intercom. "Dinner is on the table if ye've a mind tae eat."

Shanley stood and walked over to the speaker attached to the wall beside the door and pressed the button. "I most definitely have a mind to eat, Hamish. Be down in two minutes."

"That's not nearly enough time to talk about what's going on between you and Alaisdair," Ceri said as she joined her at the door to her room.

Shanley slanted her a look. "Sure, it is. There's nothing going on between Alaisdair and me. I only met the man a few hours ago."

"Uh-huh, which explains all those charged looks the two of you were sharing all afternoon and your avid interest in him."

"I have no idea what you're talking about," Shanley huffed. "Let's join the others for dinner. I'm starving. Besides, we shouldn't deny Hamish any opportunities for altering our attitudes about Conlan Manor."

The two women exchanged a conspiratorial smile and were still laughing when they entered the dining room a few minutes later.

CHAPTER TEN

SING JET LAG as an excuse, Shanley begged off early following dinner the previous evening. What she'd needed was time away from the penetrating stare of a pair of whisky-colored eyes that never strayed from her all during the meal.

Over the years, she'd dreamed on and off about a warrior matching Alaisdair Graham's description. As she thought about it, when she'd been younger, the warrior in her dreams had been younger too. And strong and handsome and utterly devoted to his brothers-in-arms. Her most recent dreams featured a man in his prime who always went down fighting whenever she dreamed of him. A man with a neatly trimmed auburn beard and mustache and long auburn hair he pulled back in a ponytail. A man who looked exactly like Alaisdair Graham.

When they'd shook hands upon meeting the previous afternoon, it had been all Shanley could do to keep herself from gasping at the electric shock arcing through her at the contact of their skin, a tingling that lingered long after they no longer touched.

Several times as she'd caught him staring at her, it seemed he was trying to place her or something, but she knew they'd never met. Someone as magnetic as Alaisdair Graham would have remained in her memory. Hell, someone as magnetic as Alaisdair Graham likely would have shared her bed.

Needing to clear her head, she decided to take a stroll in the gardens before lunch. They'd been her favorite place when she'd spent her year at Conlan Manor, and she was curious to see what Hamish had done with them, something she couldn't discern properly from her window two stories above them.

She slipped a jacket over her tan cable-knit sweater and jeans, wrapped a coral cashmere scarf around her neck, slid on her knit gloves, and exited her room. The thought of a few minutes alone in the gardens excited her, and she smiled all the way down the stairs and out the front door. Relegating thoughts of Alaisdair Graham firmly to the back of her mind, she stepped out onto the veranda and grinned up at the unusually sharp sunshine of a Scots autumn day.

Climbing the stairs from the kitchen, Alaisdair couldn't miss Shanley as she tripped lightly down the stairs from the bedrooms on the second floor, through the front foyer, and out the front door. After the arrival of the heir to Conlan Manor, Hamish had told Alaisdair of the terrible event that led to Shanley becoming Ceri's guardian years ago. Even after suffering the way Shanley had, there was something soft and alluring about her, serene and settled.

She didn't seem to want the limelight. Instead, she appeared content to step back in favor of her niece even though Conlan Manor was her heritage as well. The fact she dearly loved Ceri also attracted him. She was selfless and willing give up her dreams to raise her orphaned niece, which tugged at Alaisdair's heart.

On a whim, he decided to follow her out into the garden,

telling himself she might need the protection of a warrior outside alone this close to the festival of Samhain. Deep down he knew his reasoning was a lame excuse, but hopefully, he wouldn't have to use it.

"Nice mornin', this," he said as he walked up quietly behind her.

He hid a grin as her feet left the ground before she spun around to face him.

"Oh! What did you say?"

Her hand at her chest told him her heart might have tried to jump out of it.

"Sorry." He cleared his throat. "Nice morning. I like tae walk in the gardens all the time, but especially in the fall. The golden slant o' the sun makes the plants glow," he said, but he wasn't looking at the flowers.

In the autumn sun, Shanley's hair took on an ethereal light, like a burnished halo. His fingers itched to touch the silky strands flowing over her shoulders in smooth waves.

"Are all Scotsmen poets?" she asked with a smile.

"Nae, only the ones who find themselves in a garden with a beautiful woman, I expect." He winked.

"Are you flirting with me, Alaisdair Graham?" Her laughter drew a grin from him.

"Would ye be offended if I were?"

She tilted her head and with a finger to her lips pretended to think about his question. "No, I'm not offended. I like a handsome man flirting with me."

Blinking, she shook her head as though her answer surprised her.

Not giving her a chance to change her mind, he asked, "Shall we walk?"

With a demure nod, she fell into a leisurely stroll with him along a path that eventually took them into the heart of the garden.

After a silence, he said, "Hamish says ye stayed here fer a year before ye took on raisin' yer niece. When was that?"

What he wanted to know was how he'd missed meeting such an interesting woman back when they were both young and full of hope. As they walked beside the manicured evergreens bordering the herb beds, he buried his hands in the front pockets of his jeans and tried to ignore the occasional scent of jasmine and musk that wafted over him whenever their shoulders nearly touched.

"I accompanied my sister when she inherited the manor. I was twenty-two, so that was about eighteen years ago."

Shanley removed a glove and ran her hand along the shrubs before sniffing the fresh scent of evergreen on her fingertips. Watching her, Alaisdair balled his pocketed hands into fists to keep himself from grabbing her hand to learn how the plants smelled on her skin.

"Why dinnae yer sister stay the full year as she was meant tae dae?"

He wished he could take back the question as he watched pain travel her face before she answered. "Her husband and daughter were in America. She missed them terribly, and her husband wasn't in a position to spend a year here." She stared into the distance. "Becca stayed only the minimum three months before returning home. I'd recently finished college and had no concrete plans, so I stayed on."

"Hamish dinnae have anythin' tae dae with yer decision, did he?" he asked with a knowing grin.

"He might have suggested a year in Scotland would be a helpful experience for someone who trained to teach high school history." She smiled back. "He was right, as usual."

Alaisdair cocked a brow but said nothing.

"I needed the extra year to grow up, and the fact that I spent substantial time in Great Britain gave me street cred with people in positions to hire me."

"'Street cred?'"

A laugh bubbled out of her. "It's a term my students use. It means I had credibility when I talked about Scotland and Scots customs and literature since I'd actually lived here. My experience in Scotland set me apart from all the other graduates fresh out of college and looking for teaching positions."

"Eighteen years ago? Where was I then?" he wondered aloud.

"Pardon me?"

"I was tryin' tae work out why I wasnae around when ye were stayin' here back then. I grew up in Ullapool, so it's odd I dinnae meet ye before."

He stopped walking. Eighteen years ago, there'd been warlike unrest in Eastern Europe. With Morgan exploiting racial tensions, unscrupulous gun runners, and autocratic politicians, every available warrior in Europe had been called into service. Those who hadn't found their talismans did most of their work behind the scenes. He'd spent a rather uneventful year in Germany working surveillance from inside an ancient castle.

"I'm sorry I missed you too," Shanley blurted, interrupting his thoughts.

Alaisdair smiled.

Glancing around at where they'd wandered, he said, "Here we are in the heart o' Hamish's garden, lass. He says this is an enchanted spot full o' magic and promise." He waggled his eyebrows and grinned.

"What does he mean by that do you suppose? Is this where he grows his most powerful herbs? The ones he uses in his cooking?" She smiled back.

"Possibly," he said with a sage nod. "More likely it's because it's secluded from the prying eyes of anyone in the house below the third floor. He says this spot served lovers rather well back in the day."

Shanley looked around for a second before seating herself on the stone bench. Alaisdair sat beside her as close as possible without touching her and wrestled with his hopes.

"Though I never stopped lookin', I never did find my talisman. When I turned twenty-eight, I had nae other choice but tae go tae ground. I've helped Hamish the best I could while usin' all the protections he can invent fer me. When we heard what the Sheridans did last winter, we took it as a sign the Conlan heir was my talisman."

She trained her eyes straight ahead and said nothing. When she looked away from him, Alaisdair caught the slight downturn of her mouth.

"When Rio arrived, the twa o' them argued constantly. He never stopped badgerin' her, and I have tae admit, on more than one occasion I wanted tae challenge him and give him the comeuppance he deserved."

She pulled in a long breath and remained quiet.

"Then they discovered their connection, and the next thing I knew, I was trainin' with the world's greatest warrior under the critical eye of Scathach herself."

"Ceri tells me Rio is a particular favorite of the goddess."

Alaisdair leaned forward, his forearms on his thighs as he tried to catch her eye. "Fer good reason. I've never seen speed and skill such as that lad possesses. Anyway, the day we were training and Ceri discovered her special skill showed me beyond a doubt the two of them were fated long ago by gods who must have seen this day comin'."

When still she didn't look directly at him, he leaned a little toward her. "Yer niece and her warrior are meant tae be, and ye'll be all the safer fer it if we can help them live through whatever Morgan has planned for Samhain."

"Thank you, Alaisdair."

"Fer what?"

"Being honest. The rest of it I already knew from what Ceri

told me. She is a beautiful woman and a talisman. Of course you would—" She gasped.

He almost laughed as she nearly sprained her neck trying to see behind her. "I think there's something hiding in the hedge behind us. Can you see if I'm bleeding?" she asked in alarm as she turned her back toward him.

"Ye're not bleedin', I promise."

Again, he hadn't been able to help himself. With Shanley's insistence on not looking at him as they talked about Ceri, he could feel her hurt. Of course, his attraction to her hadn't played a role at all in what he did. *Right.*

"Are you sure? It feels like a red-hot blade broke the skin between my shoulder blades," she insisted.

"Be damned."

"Pardon?"

Alaisdair took her gently by the shoulders and turned her to face him at last. "Hamish was partly right. The fates gave me *a* Conlan heir, just not *the* Conlan heir."

Shanley stared at him, disbelief forming her pretty mouth into a perfect *O*.

"I was gobsmacked from the moment we met. Now I know why," he said as traced the pad of his finger along her hairline. "Tell me, when we shook hands in the kitchen, did ye feel somethin' like an electric shock travel up yer arm?"

Slowly, she nodded.

"I wonder how many other warriors Morgan denied their talismans that year when she kept so many of us busy fightin' a war the diplomats could have prevented if they'd had the chance," Alaisdair mused as he looked deep into the dark green forests of her eyes.

"I've dreamed about you for years. I thought I was seeing Ceri's warrior. I had no idea mine was still out there somewhere," she whispered.

"I'm six months away from my forty-second birthday. Likely, Morgan thought she had me after all. As happy as this moment is, we've probably added another layer o' danger tae an already dangerous situation."

"You sound like Hamish."

He grinned. "After all these years taegether, nae doubt he's rubbed off on me."

Tentatively, she placed a hand on his chest. The sensation of her touch penetrated the layers of clothing between them, and he had trouble following her words over the roar of blood in his ears.

"It's funny. When I was young, I fantasized that when my warrior found me, we'd have a lovely little honeymoon in some secluded place. Not be in a house full of guests with a major battle looming over us."

"The manor is attached tae a cozy cottage via a tunnel Hamish likes tae guard by keepin' his room off-limits tae everyone but me. Dae ye know if the Sheridans leave leftovers?"

"Before yesterday, I've only shared a wedding dinner with them. Why?"

"Doesnae matter. If they donnae leave us anythin', we'll fry eggs whenever we decide we're hungry later."

"What?"

No longer denying his need, he watched his fingers as he twirled a lock of silky hair around them. "I'm saying, lass, we have certain quite pleasurable obligations tae attend tae, the sooner the better fer a lot of reasons not the least of which is I havnae been able tae take my eyes off ye since we met. And donnae think fer one second age has slowed me down, nor, I doubt, has it slowed ye."

"How did you *do* that? I keep my shield up at all times!"

"Ye're my talisman. Ye're not meant tae keep secrets from me nor am I from ye. If it's wooin' ye want, how's this? Shanley Conlan, ye're an incredibly beautiful woman. Yer stillness and selflessness add tae yer loveliness. After taeday—and taenight—I'll never be the same—nor, I hope, will ye."

He pushed a strand of her hair behind her ear with one finger, savoring its silkiness and her smooth skin before he cupped her cheek in his hand. He lowered his head and touched his lips to her sweet mouth. Though he kept it butterfly soft, the kiss went on and on until she leaned into him, deepening it. He groaned low in his throat and wrapped his arms around her, pulling her to him as he parted her lips with his tongue to taste all her honeyed sugar.

She moved closer to him, pushing herself onto his lap as together they intensified the kiss. Tongues tasting and exploring, teeth taking tiny bites of lips, lips pressing and tugging, breaths catching and mingling.

Tearing his mouth away from hers at last, Alaisdair said hoarsely, "Dae ye think the others have come down tae lunch yet?"

Shanley panted. "No. Ceri would have called me if they had."

"Well then, we have a window tae escape the manor if we hurry."

"What will we say if we run into the others?" she asked as he helped her to her feet.

He couldn't hold back a big smile. "The truth o' course. It's not like any of the rest of them wouldnae understand. We're nearly the oldest warrior and talisman pair here, and so far, the latest tae the party. I intend tae remedy that directly."

Because he couldn't help himself, he pulled her flush against his body and went in for a hard kiss. "Come on, lass. Nae dawdling," Alaisdair teased as he took Shanley's hand and led her from the garden.

⚬

When they heard voices coming from the salon, they tiptoed past the open door and headed for the kitchen. There they found Rio and Ceri busy with Hamish plating roast beef, potatoes, and cabbage. Though lunch smelled heavenly as the flavors of hot beef and vegetables permeated the air, Alaisdair and Shanley had a different hunger to assuage.

Never relinquishing his hold on her hand, Alaisdair guided Shanley toward the hallway. They nearly made it to Hamish's room when Ceri called out. "There you are! I thought you were napping off jet lag, so I thought I'd wait to wake you until right before we served lunch, but you're up," she said brightly before she blinked at Alaisdair. "Is something wrong?"

"Naethin' that spendin' some time alone with the lass won't cure, eh old friend?" Hamish asked as he looked up from slicing fresh bread.

Ceri glanced from Alaisdair to Hamish and back to Shanley, who blushed. Ceri turned a puzzled glance at Rio who burst out laughing.

"No kidding? Congratulations, you two. Took you long enough. 'Course, being separated by a continent and an ocean might cause certain delays." Rio winked at Alaisdair.

"Jumped the gun, lad—again." Hamish emitted a long-suffering sigh. "Cannae be helped now." He went back to preparing food. "Ye best be takin' care o' business, I expect. We'll put somethin' aside fer ye. Ye know where the key is."

"Sorry, Hamish. I know ye wanted me tae wait, but ye dinnae see her in the glow o' the sun. Even *you* couldnae resisted such a lovely vision," Alaisdair said, pulling Shanley into his side.

"Oh my! Shanley? Are you and Alaisdair—?" Ceri gaped at them.

Shanley stepped forward and squeezed Ceri's hand. "Yes, love. My warrior has finally found me, and we have some things to do," she said, her tone gentle.

Ceri moved to hug her, but Rio stayed her. "Now is not the time, sweetheart. She'll talk to you later."

"With Scathach insistin' on trainin' taemorrow, ye can count on seein' yer aunt then," Hamish said. His eyes on Shanley and Alaisdair, he tilted his head toward the hallway. "The twa o' ye had best make the most o' what's left o' taeday. Ye'll know when ye're needed at *An Teallach*." Carrying a platter of vegetables, he headed toward the stairs.

"Thanks, auld friend. Rio, Ceri, give our regrets tae the rest o' yer family. Nae doubt they'll understand," Alaisdair said with a grin he could no longer contain. Tugging Shanley's hand, he led her down the hall to Hamish's room.

Rio stepped around the corner to sneak a glance into the old druid's private space. Knowing how badly Rio had wanted to check out Hamish's rooms, especially when the old man denied him, Alaisdair obligingly held the door open long enough to give Rio a good look. With a grin directed at his warrior brother, Alaisdair closed the door and led Shanley through Hamish's rooms to the tunnel connecting the manor to his cottage.

Chapter Eleven

HANLEY BARELY NOTICED the odd assortment of old furniture with which Hamish decorated his apartment as Alaisdair hustled her through the main room. The strange aroma of drying plants and incense wafted to her nose, but she didn't have time to determine exactly what made up the weird, though not unpleasant smell. Alaisdair's big hand encompassed hers in a firm hold, comforting and right. Though she'd never admit it aloud, she rather liked being whisked away by a warrior eager to spend time alone with her.

He let go of her long enough to retrieve a key from the pocket of his jeans and insert it into the lock on the heavy wooden door on the far side of the room. The door itself appeared ancient as though it had been built at the time of the manor itself, but the handle and locking mechanisms were modern. His key turned the lock easily, yet he added an odd flick of the wrist as the tumblers dropped into place.

Pulling open the heavy door, he flipped a switch illuminating the floor on either side of a tunnel with a runway of soft blue light. The lights let one follow the tunnel without being blinded by white light, allowing one's eyes to adjust quickly when entering the passageway. He tugged her behind him before pulling the door shut and relocking it.

Carved of solid slate, the tunnel held no heat. Shanley shivered involuntarily and walked closely beside Alaisdair.

"How far is it to your cottage?" she asked through chattering teeth.

"Not far. Ye'll get used tae the cold after ye've used the tunnel a few times."

"Why do you stay in the cottage?"

"Hamish and I are good friends, but even good friends need time apart."

Shanley caught a note of despair in Alaisdair's tone and squeezed his hand.

"Didn't we see your room when Ceri took us on the tour yesterday?"

"Aye, and we'll be stayin' in the manor after taenight, at least until after the fireworks at Samhain. But I thought ye might like some privacy our first night taegether. I know I would," he said with a grin she couldn't see but could definitely hear.

"Nae need tae turn all pink, lass. Bondin' is expected between a warrior and his talisman as soon after he discovers her as he can possibly arrange. Ye know that," Alaisdair said with a chuckle.

"You can't possibly know I'm blushing."

"I can almost feel yer face heating the air between us."

"Alaisdair!"

He met her indignation with a chuckle.

She sighed. "I didn't expect to have the experience, and back when I did expect it, I always thought it would be private. Taking me to your cottage when everyone else at the manor is at lunch feels like a public declaration of what is going to happen between us rather than the quiet moment I envisioned when I was young."

Shanley tugged at his hand to slow him down.

"Sorry, lass." He adjusted his stride. "Considerin' what a robust group those Sheridans are and the hard time they were givin' yer niece when ye arrived, I donnae think we're goin' tae escape some good-natured commentary nae matter when our bondin' time happens. Takin' ye tae the cottage seemed the most private thing tae do."

He stopped abruptly and turned to her. She barreled into his hard chest, and he wrapped his arms around her. "Besides, I want tae see what it's like tae entertain my woman in the one place I've come tae call my own in the world. Ye wouldnae deprive me of that now, would ye?"

"Of course not." She hugged him back. "It just would have been nice to have been discovered without an audience," she whispered into the heavy wool of his sweater.

"I'll make it worth yer while, I promise." His smile lit up the gloom of the passageway.

Taking her hand again, he tugged her along behind him. They arrived at another door, one of equal weight and age as the one at the opposite end of the tunnel. Again, she watched as he unlocked the door with a smooth motion followed by a flick of his wrist she couldn't quite follow. If she was going to use this route, he was going to have to teach her how to unlock the doors.

As they stepped into his cottage, he turned on a lamp on a table placed strategically beside the door. The soft light illuminated a cozy sitting room with heavy woolen rugs covering a floor of slate flagstone. The furnishings were surprisingly modern. Why she'd expected something more antique, she couldn't say, but the chocolate-colored suede couch and recliner resting at angles facing the fireplace invited her to sit. The polished mahogany end tables flanking the couch added richness to the room. The heavy mahogany coffee table was littered with magazines about travel and weaponry and history, giving her a glimpse of what interested her warrior.

Wrought iron lamps with ivory-colored shades sat on the end tables, while a floor lamp of the same style overlooked the recliner. As Shanley stepped farther into the room, Alaisdair switched on more lamps. From the corner of her eye, she caught him watching her, and she thought he held his breath as he did so.

Tracing her fingers over the books on the bookshelves built into the wall on one side of the fireplace, she was relieved she'd be forever knit to an educated man who apparently read widely. His library contained history, poetry, and science books as well as a few popular paperback thrillers—things she too enjoyed reading in her spare time.

Tearing herself away from his books, she noticed a framed painting of Conlan Manor hanging above the mantel on the fireplace.

"It's part of the protections Hamish placed on the cottage. The connection tae the manor adds another layer of safety tae this house. Besides, it's a rather pretty picture, isn't it?"

"Yes. But can't you see the manor from here?"

Alaisdair stood beside her as she gazed at the painting. "Only the back of it. This paintin' includes the gardens, and that's the secret tae its power, I think."

"Of course. The connection to the earth. I should have seen that."

"Let me show ye the kitchen and the rest o' the cottage," he said, taking her hand again. Since he'd discovered their connection, it seemed he couldn't go long without touching her, not that she minded. She rather liked touching him too.

Through an archway to the left of the door to the tunnel, he led her to the kitchen. Brick red handles accented white oak cupboards above black granite countertops. The stove and refrigerator were the retro rounded design popular in the sixties, but updated versions judging from their larger size.

The red-and-white gingham curtains over the window above

the sink tied the room together and matched the seat covers on the heavy oak chairs arranged around the oak table in the corner of the room. A butcher-block island separated the cooking area from the eating area. Though small, the space was comfortable. Shanley fell in love immediately.

"Ye like it?"

"It's so cozy."

An expression of relief flitted across his face. "I've heard if a woman likes the kitchen, she'll like the whole house."

"Is that right?" she drawled.

He shrugged, but she caught a subtle red hue riding high on his cheekbones. He led her back through the living room and down a short hallway. Stopping outside a door, he motioned for her to look inside the bathroom, a tiny utilitarian affair with a shower, a freestanding sink, and a toilet. A medicine cabinet above the sink appeared to be the only storage space in the room. She slanted him a disconcerted look, and he pointed out the linen closet across the hall from the bathroom, which only slightly mollified her.

"I know ye lasses like tae have yer space for yer toilette, but ye have tae remember, this cottage was built at the same time as the manor. A gamekeeper's lodge with an outside privy. Findin' even that much space fer indoor plumbin' was quite an undertakin'."

The defensiveness in Alaisdair's tone set off alarm bells in Shanley's head.

"This is an ancient home. I had tae fashion this room out of a closet. The shower is much bigger than it looks from the outside though. Ye'll see."

"You installed it?"

"I did, lass."

With a game smile, she said, "You're right. It's a huge improvement over heading outside or back up the passageway to the manor."

Alaisdair tilted his head as though trying to decide if he believed her before he took Shanley's hand again and coaxed her a few more steps down the hall to his bedroom.

She stopped short at the sight of the monster four-poster bed dominating the space.

"I rescued that from the refurbishin' session that took place at the manor before Ceri arrived."

"Did all those pillows and the quilt come from the manor too?"

"Nae. A local artist made 'em. A gift from Hamish fer when I—"

"When you what?"

"Never mind. Now is not the time fer that story. Might put a damper on the mood."

She considered his remark and decided to save her curiosity for later. Nodding at the tall lampstands bracketing the bed, she asked, "Do you like to read in bed?"

"Every night. Except maybe not so much anymore."

The wolfish grin on his face heated Shanley from the roots of her hair to the soles of her feet.

Taking a turn around the room, she observed an oversized antique wardrobe serving as Alaisdair's closet. A freestanding oval mirror flanked the wardrobe. As she continued her visual tour, she saw a window opposite the wardrobe, its curtains matching the muted heather, taupe, and green of the quilt and draping gracefully aside. After the tunnel, she expected the interior of the cottage to be constructed entirely of stone, but the walls in the living room were pine while plaster covered the walls of the rest of the house, giving it an airy lightness.

Except for the size of the bathroom, she loved his home. As she came to that realization, she wondered what he would think of her apartment if he ever got the chance to see it.

"About yer apartment—what dae ye mean if I ever get the chance tae see it? Ye donnae think ye'll invite me tae the States?"

She fisted her hands on her hips. "How did you *do* that? I'm sure I had my shield up."

Alaisdair chuckled. "I'm yer warrior, Shanley. We're connected. Ye know as well as I dae that we'll hear each other's thoughts. Now about that invitation—" He rested his hands heavily on her shoulders and waited.

"I was only thinking that if all Hamish implies is true, we have to live through Samhain before we can make any future plans." She stared at his massive chest. "Of course, if we do, then we'll have to have a long conversation about what's going to happen since I'm a Yank and you're a Scot. I like living in America, and I imagine you like living here. We'll have some compromising to do if we live through the weekend."

"Undoubtedly, ye're right, lass. But I'm not interested in lookin' past taeday. Everythin' I ever wanted and stopped hopin' tae have is standin' right in front of me, and I intend tae make ye so happy the rest takes care of itself." He stepped to within a breath of her. "Now, where were we out in the garden?"

Pulling her gently into his arms, he nibbled at her bottom lip, coaxing her to kiss him. His neatly trimmed beard and mustache intrigued her, and she cupped his face in one hand and followed his lead, kissing him fully, the soft texture of his beard in the palm of her hand adding a sensual dimension she didn't even know she liked until that moment.

Tightening his arms around her, Alaisdair kissed her endlessly, drawing Shanley deeper into his embrace. At last, she opened for him. When he plunged his tongue into her mouth, she lost herself. Rubbing her body against his, she desperately wished she hadn't worn so many clothes.

Pulling away, he smiled down at her. "There's a remedy fer that, lass."

He proceeded to show her by unbuttoning her sweater, his knuckles leaving a trail of heat on her skin. She tuned in to his touch so entirely she barely noticed he'd breached her shield again. Instead, she held her breath as he pushed her sweater over her shoulders and down her arms before letting it drop to the floor.

He slid his big hands up the smooth skin of her torso, and she shivered at his touch, anticipating where his hands might go next. The calluses on his fingertips and palms only excited her more, and she wanted to feel them everywhere on her.

Smiling into her eyes, he slipped his hands behind her to unclasp her bra before sliding the ivory lace confection slowly off her body. As he stepped back for a better look at her, she resisted an instinctive response to cover herself while trying unsuccessfully to squelch the blush stealing over her chest and cheeks.

"I've never seen anythin' so beautiful as ye are, Shanley."

It took her a moment to realize she heard him in her head. He sat on the bed and tugged her to stand between his legs. Bending his head to her chest, he lapped at her erect nipple before sucking it deep into his mouth while he explored every inch of her back with his magical hands. She gasped her pleasure, arching into him as she buried her fingers in his hair and held him to her. He licked and kissed and sucked her nipple, driving her wild, her need pulsing insistently between her legs.

"I don't think I can take anymore, Alaisdair," she whispered.

"Sure ye can, lass." Humor danced in his voice as he transferred his attentions to her other breast.

Her knees went to water. The heaviness low in her belly echoed in the dampness in her panties. It was clear he knew his effect on her before he kissed his way down her middle to the waistband of her jeans.

Carefully, he unbuttoned and unzipped and eased her jeans down the length of her legs. He grinned up at her when he revealed ivory lace bikini briefs and, after running his hands over them, left them on her. Her shoes impeded his progress, so he stood and lifted her onto the bed to finish his task.

Gazing at her legs, Alaisdair grinned happily. "I am one lucky man."

He knelt down to unlace his work boots and made short work of his jeans and boxers before tugging his wool sweater over his head. Shanley's body heated and melted at the sight of her heavily muscled and toned warrior whose intentions for her jutted up between his legs.

"Ye're not afraid, lass?" he inquired, flicking a glance down at himself. "As my talisman, ye need tae know exactly what tae expect."

She couldn't help but stare at his impressive erection. "You're stunning." Reaching up to touch him, she knew instinctively he'd be everything she could ever want.

"Shanley."

The bed sagged under his weight as he lowered himself beside her and took her into his arms for another soul-searing kiss. Shanley couldn't understand why he hadn't removed all her clothes earlier. She squirmed and tried to reach her panties, but he stayed her with a hand on her wrist.

"Not yet, lass. This is our first time. I want tae remember every detail."

"Please, Alaisdair. You're killing me."

"Isnae that the auld saying? Making love is like dying the little death?" he teased.

"You've driven me totally wild, and now you want to be a philosopher?" She flopped back against the pillows. "I'll never survive this."

He chuffed out a low laugh before she turned the tables and measured his length in her hands. She smiled when he gasped as she smoothed her fingers over the silky skin covering his hardness, a texture and sensation she had no doubt would fascinate her endlessly. Alaisdair let her have her way for a bit before he slid down her length to kiss and lick her through her panties, his caress sending her over the edge. Arching against him, she lost herself in his ministrations, screaming his name.

"Yes!" he yelled in triumph.

Before Shanley could come back to herself, he peeled off the sexy barrier to their desire, settled himself in the vee of her thighs, and joined her to him in one smooth, deep stroke. She cried out in wonder at the incredible way he stretched her, filled her, and she wrapped her arms and legs around him, holding him deep inside her.

"I thought I'd prepared fer bonding with my talisman." He groaned as he stroked her. "What ye're showin' me, lass, is reality far surpasses my dreams. Ye're so much more than everything I've ever wanted."

As they moved together, it occurred to her the gods knew exactly what they were doing when they determined the pairings of talismans and warriors. Nothing else in the world could compare with sharing herself with her mate. Then she couldn't think anymore as she reveled in the sensations of coming together as one with her warrior.

CHAPTER TWELVE

UCH LATER, ALAISDAIR leaned up on one elbow to look at the incredible woman for whom he'd waited his whole life and knew Shanley was worth every trial, every test he'd endured to live long enough to find her. Her golden strawberry-colored hair fanned across the pillow in a halo highlighted by the lamp he'd turned on to see her after twilight turned to dusk when he took her the second time. Her creamy skin glowed in the lamplight. Her slightly parted lips, bruised a deep rose from his kissing, invited him to kiss her again. But he knew where that would lead, and he wanted to let her rest awhile longer.

Carefully, he eased himself from the bed, grabbed a flannel robe from the wardrobe, and shrugged it on as he walked down the hall to the living room to build up the fire. When it crackled to his satisfaction, he headed into the kitchen to prepare a meal. Though Hamish said he would save them dinner, Alaisdair loathed leaving Shanley for even the few minutes it would take him to walk to the manor and back with leftovers.

Staring into his fridge, he decided breakfast would have to do. After dropping some sausages into a pan to fry, he sliced tomatoes in half and slid them under the broiler. While he tried to decide whether to toast or fry the bread, Shanley padded into the kitchen in nothing but her socks and one of his button-down shirts. With her sleep-tousled hair, she looked much better to him than breakfast.

"What time is it?" she asked, her raspy voice not yet recovered from sleep and the cries his lovemaking had called from her.

"Around eight. We missed dinner at the manor, so I thought I'd make breakfast fer dinner here. D'ye like yer bread toasted or fried?"

"At home, I never eat it fried, but fried tastes better when I'm here."

Her answer pleased him, and he put a heavy pan on the stove to fry the bread.

"Can I help?"

"Ye can set the table. Ye'll find everythin' ye need in the cupboards by the fridge. Maybe ye could also put the kettle on."

Wordlessly, Shanley went about her tasks while Alaisdair checked the sausages. In easy silence, they worked together to prepare the meal before sitting down together at the kitchen table.

"We did that rather well, lass."

"Make dinner or make love?"

Her sense of humor was something else he liked about her.

"Aye," he returned with a grin. "We seem tae have come tae a rather quick understandin', the two o' us."

She smiled at him and tucked into her meal. While she ate, he studied her and marveled anew at his good fortune. *"Ye were more than worth the wait, lass."*

Her eyes widened in surprise. Then those eyes sparkled mischievously. "You better eat well, mister, because later on, you're going to need it."

His laughter filled the cottage. "Them's brave words, lass. I cannae wait tae see how ye back them up."

Reaching across the table, he covered her hand with his. "Discoverin' ye tae be my talisman has already made me the happiest man on earth." He squeezed her hand. "As long as I live, I donnae think I'll ever experience anythin' as astoundingly beautiful as bondin' with ye."

Turning her hand over in his, she laced her fingers in his and smiled.

"Ye're everythin' this auld warrior ever wanted. Beautiful, educated, loyal—and secretly naughty."

Shanley tilted her head. "Naughty? Whatever do you mean?"

Alaisdair chuckled. "Aye, naughty, lass. Was it only a few minutes ago ye were challengin' me on my stamina?"

"I have no idea what you're talking about." She batted her eyes at him.

"Ye're on notice that I intend tae take the mickey out o' ye just as much as ye dae tae me."

"Yeah? I'm going to enjoy this relationship." She grinned and returned her attention to her meal. "You know, the teasing and all."

"I know ye are."

Her eyes flew to his.

"I already dae."

She quirked a brow, and he glanced down at his plate where he discovered he'd eaten everything.

"Are ye good? Dae ye want anythin' else?"

Shanley sopped up egg yolk with the last of her fried bread, popped the morsel in her mouth, and shook her head. After swallowing, she said, "Those last two sausages are all yours."

Grinning happily, he speared the sausages with his fork and transferred them to his plate. "Thanks, lass. Just ensurin' my stamina meets yer exactin' demands, ye see."

"As a good warrior should."

Laughter roared out of him.

After settling himself down, he said, "We're well matched, Shanley Conlan."

"We most certainly are." She thoughtfully sipped her tea and peered over the rim of her mug at him. "I would have enjoyed the additional thirteen or so years together that Morgan denied us, but I feel lucky to have you in my life now. As much as you impressed me in my dreams, the reality is even better."

At the mention of her dreams, Alaisdair's meal turned to lead in his stomach.

"Wait. What dreams?"

"Finish your breakfast, or dinner or whatever," she laughed, but it was hollow. "Then I'll tell you."

✍

In silence, they worked together to clean up the kitchen, the teasing camaraderie they'd enjoyed lost in those two words—my dreams. Shanley dreamed of him? What did that mean? The gods never revealed a warrior to his talisman before he tried his sign on her, did they?

He topped off their mugs of tea and motioned for her to follow him into the living room. Seating himself on the couch, he patted the place beside him.

When she sat, he slid his arm along the back of the cushions behind her and leaned toward her. With a gentle finger on her chin, he turned her to face him.

"Tell me about these dreams, lass."

"They feel like premonitions, especially those that come on when I'm awake. I thought I was seeing Ceri's warrior. But over the years, I've seen an auburn-haired warrior who looked an awful lot like you."

"How many years?"

She sipped her tea and stared at the flames dancing in the grate in front of them. When she blinked up at him, he watched as a revelation came into her eyes. "Since the year I lived here at Conlan Manor," she whispered, and he thought he detected a tremor of fear in her voice.

"Did Hamish try tae talk ye intae stayin' longer?"

"He did, but if I wanted to find a teaching position at home, which I did, I had to leave when my year at the manor was up. There was also the issue of Becca asking me if I could help with Ceri." She smoothed the hem of his shirt where it rested on the top of her thigh. "Morgan had escalated confrontations between civilian gangs to draw out warriors. Things were tense at home, and Becca wanted another talisman with Ceri whenever she was called out to help Ian." Her voice took on a faraway tone. "Which was often."

"I'm sorry fer yer loss, Shanley."

A sad smile pressed her lips. "Thanks. Even though it was a long time ago, Becca and I were close. I miss her every day."

Alaisdair gently took the mug from her hands and placed it on the table in front of them. Leaning back, he traced the contours of her face with his finger. "Tell me about these premonitions o' yers."

"At first, I watched this warrior taking on civilians in some sort of war zone. It made no sense because the US wasn't actively fighting any wars in which warriors would be called to help."

"Yeah, but the unrest that led tae the partitions in Eastern Europe were happenin' then."

Looking down, he threaded his fingers through the silky strands of her hair, letting her know he was with her, yet trying not to crowd her as she grasped what he said. Those beautiful green eyes widened in understanding as he caught her stare in his peripheral vision.

He leaned in closer as her voice dropped. "You were there, in Eastern Europe. Ceri told me something about that."

"Aye, I was. Then the Irish Republican Army decided tae give it one last go before cooler heads finally prevailed, so I was called back tae the Isle tae lend a hand in the heart of England." Taking her hand, he watched himself entangle his fingers with hers. "I returned tae Ullapool awhile after that."

She quirked a brow. "You expected to find your talisman here, on the edge of Scotland?"

"Not really. I made several trips tae warrior gatherin's all over Great Britain. I spent a lot of time in Ireland. On my twenty-eighth birthday, I found my way home tae Ullapool, got myself well and truly pissed at the pub, and woke up the next day in Hamish's apartment."

"You've lived here ever since?"

After drawing in a long breath and letting it out slowly, he said, "Until Ceri arrived, I hadn't stepped foot off Conlan lands in over thirteen years."

She stared at their entwined fingers. "I'm sorry I misjudged you. I can't imagine how confining these years have been."

For several minutes, they mourned the lost years in silence. He stroked her hand and let it go so he could wrap her in his arms and hold her close. "It's all good now, Shanley. In the short time I've known ye, ye've made it clear tae me ye were worth the sacrifice."

"Oh, Alaisdair."

Burying her face in his chest, she clung to him. Dampness on his skin alerted him to her distress.

"Donnae cry fer me." He pulled back and dried the tears on her cheeks with his thumbs. "Though I couldnae help my warrior brothers the way I could have if I'd had my talisman, I still found ways tae work in the community." Holding her face in his hands, he stared deep into her eyes. "Sometimes at odd times of the day, a warmth stole over me, like someone was watching out fer me. That's when ye were dreamin' of me, I expect." He grinned at her. "Though there were a few years where those feelin's were few and far between."

"After I reached my early thirties, I thought the chances of my warrior finding me had passed. About then, the premonitions dropped off. You must have gone to ground by then."

"And now?"

Shanley busied herself with her tea. In the short time they'd been together, he'd learned to spot her tells. "Lass." He didn't mean the hard edge in his voice, but now was not the time for holding back.

She closed her eyes tightly, and he noticed how her knuckles whitened as she gripped the mug in her hands. Still, she remained silent. When he thought he'd have to find a way to force it out of her, she began to speak.

Keeping her eyes on the fire crackling in front of them, she said, "Lately, I've been watching as Morgan sets rogues upon you. You're always outnumbered, you always take a few with you, and you—"

She swallowed hard.

"And I—"

The distress he saw in her eyes when they flew to his both heartened and terrified him.

"You always fall."

Alaisdair peeled her fingers from her cup and set it back on the table. Instinctively knowing she needed the reassurance, he gathered her in his arms and pulled her onto his lap.

"For the past several months, I've awakened every day with tears on my face," she whispered into the crook of his neck.

"I'm here, Shanley. Now that I've found ye, I have nae intentions of goin' anywhere. We both waited tae long and lost tae much tae lose each other now."

They tightened their arms around each other and held on.

Chapter Thirteen

"WE COULD WHIP up breakfast here again. I don't mind," Shanley said.

The exaggerated batting of her eyes twitched a grin out of him. "Lass, ye know we're goin' tae have tae face them eventually. Might as well get it over with."

Another thought occurred to him. "Yer reluctance tae join yer niece and her new family wouldnae have a little somethin' tae dae with the way ye might have been teasin' her when ye arrived, would it?"

A puff of air fluffed the bangs on her forehead, and he couldn't help but enjoy the rosy tinge blooming high on her cheeks.

"When I didn't think I had a snowball's chance in hell of experiencing it, it was easy to dish it out. Now the shoe is on my foot, and I'll admit, I'm not too keen on wearing it."

Alaisdair cupped her face in his hands and stared into the endless forests of her eyes. "Shanley. I just experienced the greatest afternoon, night, and mornin' of my life. Tae be honest, I'm rather excited about joinin' the others. All of them, except fer Hamish of course, know somethin' of what we've shared.

Finally, I get tae join the party." Because he couldn't help himself, he stroked her heated cheeks with the pads of his thumbs. "And so dae ye."

She dropped her head onto his chest. Taking advantage, he wrapped her in his arms. He could understand her embarrassment—to a point. After all these years, she never expected to be in this position. It would have been nice if he could have discovered her years ago when the experience would have likely been more private. Still. In the warrior community, she was every bit as potent as he now that she was a bonded talisman. The teasing would only serve to cement that fact.

As they entered the kitchen at the manor via Hamish's apartment, Shanley tried again.

"We can grab some porridge from that pot on the stove"— she indicated with a nod—"and eat breakfast here in the kitchen." She'd tugged him to a stop at the bottom of the stairs and started with the puppy dog eyes again.

He nearly choked as he stifled a laugh at the comical look of hope on her face.

Rubbing his thumb over her hand reassuringly, he said, "Nae doubt Hamish has already sensed our presence inside the manor. Nae matter how ye look at it, lass, we're committed."

He punctuated the double entendre with a hard kiss that— because it was with his talisman and she was Shanley—wasted no time morphing into something dark and erotic. At last, Alaisdair reacted to the supernatural currents rippling through him, belatedly understanding they came from someone in the manor beyond his talisman. When he let them up for air, her eyes reflected the same desire coursing through his blood. Standing in the circle of his arms, no doubt she could feel his hard length against her soft body.

She swallowed. Loudly. "All right, Alaisdair, this is a good alternative to breakfast."

He grinned at her. "Nae sense in puttin' off the inevitable."

She slanted him a look before sighing resignedly.

The smile remained on his face when he opened the massive double oak doors to the dining room. Somehow, the familiar room appeared utterly new, like he'd never seen it before. His eyes flashed over the long hall to the fireplace at the far end where Fianna Conlan's portrait surveyed the room and all who entered it. It seemed to him the benign smile on Fianna's face warmed at the sight of him. Family portraits and highland landscapes decorated the dark oak paneling lining the room. He flicked a glance at his favorite, the portrait of Pearce Conlan, the rock of the warrior side of the clan and his distant uncle. Somehow, it seemed he too welcomed Alaisdair fully into the clan.

The dining table designed to seat at least forty warriors took up the middle of the room. Flanking the table on the end nearest the doors sat the entirety of the Sheridan family with Hamish taking his usual place at the foot of the table facing the massive fireplace at the other end of the hall.

It took him several seconds to puzzle out the difference before it occurred to him—he belonged here now. With the discovery of his talisman, he could take his rightful place in the Conlan clan and in the warrior community in general. His heart swelled in gratitude and joy, the smile on his face widening as conversation stopped abruptly when he and Shanley entered the room.

Alaisdair barely registered the smells of breakfast—sausages, fried eggs, toast, porridge, and coffee—before the onslaught began.

Rowan Sheridan launched the opening salvo. "It appears you're still functional, Alaisdair. We were kinda worried, what with your advanced age and all."

He felt Shanley pull back, but he tugged her closer to him and waggled his eyebrows at Rowan.

"Like good whisky, some things get better with age. It's a lesson ye should learn," Alaisdair returned good-humoredly.

Across the table from Rowan, Owen Sheridan saluted him with his cup. "Well said, Alaisdair. Well said."

Beside Rowan, Rio crossed his arms and regarded Alaisdair. "Huh. I've heard some whiskys lose their bite with age."

"Donnae know which whisky ye've been drinkin', Rio, but after tastin' this vintage, Shanley dinnae want tae stop with one dram. Did ye, lass?"

"*Alaisdair!*"

She buried her face between his shoulder blades as the room exploded in guffaws.

"This lot dinnae think we could keep up, lass. Appears we've surpassed them. Nae shame in that," he said over his shoulder before he pulled her around in front of him and kissed her soundly in front of the whole family.

Loud applause approved his antics.

"Bravo, Alaisdair."

"That's the spirit, man."

"He certainly fits in with this bunch."

"No doubt he has it in him with his sword arm too."

"Fine whisky. Ha. Shanley scored a warrior poet."

Alaisdair kissed his way to Shanley's ear where he whispered, "Ye see, lass. We're officially part of the family now."

"I'll expect to enjoy *several* drams of your fine whisky later, warrior," she whispered back.

Sensing her lips stretch into a smile against the skin of his jaw buoyed him. He tightened his arms around her for one more second, reassuring both of them. Stepping out of her embrace, he slid his hands down her arms to catch hers, grinned broadly, and said, "Dae ye think this lot left us anythin' fer breakfast?"

"I certainly hope so. We need to replenish our energy after"— she caught herself and cleared her throat—"so much *uisge beatha.*"

Seated at the end of the table nearest the door, Owen Sheridan must have heard her. "Water of life," he said, laughing. "No truer words were ever spoken."

He winked at Sian, his wife, before nodding toward his three sons seated down the benches from them.

From his place at the end of the table, Hamish joined the conversation. "Good tae see ye, Alaisdair, Shanley." He glanced at an imaginary watch on his wrist. "But it's comin' up on afternoon." His eyes twinkled. "So, the twa o' ye should eat somethin' quick. We're lookin' at a long trainin' at *An Teallach* taeday. Scathach will likely have some nasty reprimands tae hand if we keep her waitin'."

Hamish's warning sobered the whole assembly.

"Hamish is right about that," Riley Sheridan said with a grimace as he rubbed his hand over his biceps.

"True that, bro. There's nothing fun about training with an angry goddess," Rowan said.

Shanley gifted Alaisdair with a relieved glance as Hamish's admonishment doused the risqué comments like a bucket of cold water.

At the buffet, they loaded their plates with eggs, beans, sausages, fried bread, and broiled tomatoes. Taking places farther down the table past the rest of the family, they savored their breakfast as much as they could while the others carried their dishes to the kitchen. By the time they finished breakfast, the Sheridans were ready to go. Though they wished to linger over their meal and each other, there was no time for that.

Knowing the agenda for the day, Alaisdair had brought along his leathers and claymore, leaving them in the kitchen before they went upstairs. Shanley had dressed in jeans, a T-shirt, and a sweater, anticipating she'd need to strip down during the training session but would need something warm afterward. They ate their meal in companionable silence before carrying their dishes to the kitchen.

The others went to their rooms to retrieve the items they

needed for training, and everyone met in the hall to confirm the plan.

"I admit tae feelin' a might uncomfortable with ye ridin' with us tae *An Teallach*, Shanley. I fear ye're as much a target fer Morgan as Ceri, but since ye havnae been tae the trainin' room in years, it seems tae risky tae let ye try visualizin' yerself there taeday," Hamish said.

"It's fine, Hamish. I didn't have any premonitions that took place in the early afternoon. Everything I've seen has happened late in the day," Shanley said.

The normally unflappable Hamish Buchanan nearly jumped out of his skin at Shanley's casual revelation. "Ye've been dreamin' o' Alaisdair already?"

"I've been dreaming about him off and on for going on thirteen years," she said. "For the past two years, it's been more often than not. I thought I was seeing Ceri's warrior." She stepped closer to Alaisdair. "Turns out, I was seeing my own." She directed her last words at Alaisdair with a smile.

"So, ye've been havin' premonitions, no' actual prophecies?"

Shanley scrunched up her face in question. "They're not the same?"

"Afraid no'." Hamish's expression was as serious as Alaisdair had ever seen it.

The Sheridans had gathered around them, listening closely. When Alaisdair glanced over Shanley's head, he saw Sian Sheridan almost vibrating as she stared single-mindedly at Rio, her son and Ceri's warrior.

Feeling the trembling of his own talisman, Alaisdair rubbed a reassuring hand up and down her spine.

"What do you mean?" Shanley demanded.

"When Ceri has a prophecy, no one can reach her. They come on without warning when she's wide awake. It's terrifying to watch her have one," Owen patiently explained, eyeing Ceri with sympathy.

"You've seen Ceri have a prophecy? How can that be?"

Alaisdair interrupted Shanley's morose thoughts. *"Donnae berate yerself, lass. Ye did the best ye could with what yer niece let ye see. Knowin' her, she dinnae want tae alarm ye by lettin' ye know her shield wasnae strong."*

He had to brace himself as she slumped against him. Her pain radiated through him as she stared sorrowfully at her niece.

"I'm sorry, Ceri. You were always so good at shielding me, I thought—"

Ceri reached out and patted her hand. "It's fine, Shanley. Really. You did everything you could for me, became the mom I needed. I owe you everything."

Rio stepped forward and touched Shanley's arm. "As do I. If you hadn't done the great job you did with her, I may never have met Ceri, bonded with her, resisted the fate Morgan tries to subject all warriors to." He smiled at her. "Thank you, Shanley. For Ceri."

He wrapped his arm around his talisman and pulled her close. Ceri beamed up at him before turning a toned-down version of her smile on Shanley.

"We can finish this conversation at the trainin' room," Hamish said, turning on his heel to lead the group down the stairs and out to the cars waiting in the car park.

The Sheridans and Conlans looked around at each other before Rowan burst out laughing. "Guess someone needs to be in charge," he said, staring at Hamish's retreating back. "Come on Pixie-girl. Best not keep Scathach waiting." He clasped hands with his wife Alyssa and followed Hamish. Two by two, the others did the same, leaving Alaisdair and Shanley alone in the middle of the foyer.

Sliding his fingers into her hair, Alaisdair held her and stared into the eyes he knew would mesmerize him for the rest of his days. "Judging from the woman she is, ye did well raisin' Ceri." He cupped her jaw and smoothed the pad of his thumb over her cheek because he couldn't help but touch her.

She nodded, but he didn't miss the doubt in her eyes.

Pulling her close, he rested his face on her hair, breathed in the musky way her scent changed his perception of his woodsy soap, which was all he'd had in the shower for her earlier. How could he have anticipated discovering his talisman yesterday? He smiled at the thought before jerking his attention back to its proper place.

"All will be well. Ye'll see."

Shanley hugged him back like she wanted to absorb his strength and optimism before hand in hand, they descended the stairs to join the others.

CHAPTER FOURTEEN

SCATHACH STARTED THE day in a cranky mood, judging from the way she launched into training the warriors, especially Alaisdair and Rio. Less than an hour into the training session, all the warriors except for Owen had removed their shirts, their torsos running with sweat.

Which was not to say Owen wasn't exerting himself. At the edge of the room, he worked with Ceri on her shield, a sheen of perspiration shining on their foreheads.

Sian, Alyssa, and Lynnette, Riley's wife, worked with their husbands as Scathach launched attack after attack. From the sidelines, Shanley watched the warriors spar. Alaisdair's honed muscles flexed and bunched as he thrust and parried with blindingly fast Rio Sheridan. Shanley marveled at their skill and wondered at Scathach's temper. Perhaps if she and Alaisdair had had the proper time to bond, she could be helping him meet the exacting standards of their divine warrior trainer. Since she didn't have a clue about her special skill, she turned away from the mock battles in front of her and refamiliarized herself with the scenes of ancient battles won that had been painted over the surfaces of the rock.

Long ago, warriors hollowed out a room deep in the center of *An Teallach*, the tallest mountain on the shores of Loch Broom. When Shanley had visited years earlier, she'd admired the back-breaking effort it must have taken for men with crude pickaxes and sledgehammers to quarry out the vast space inside a mountain born of slate and basalt. The effort had been necessary. The ancient children of the earth, the *Tuatha Dè Danann*, must have their underground spaces in which to train and shelter if necessary. As part of that lineage, modern-day warriors returned to their safe places for the same reasons.

Lost in her thoughts, she skimmed the paintings until she wandered directly in front of a depiction of Tristan taking on the *Morhaus* in the battle for Isolde of Ireland. When she stopped in front of the painting, a searing pain behind her eyes assaulted her, knocking her to her knees.

Clutching at her head, Shanley watched in horror as Alaisdair took on Morgan's champion, a giant creature with otherworldly strength and no ethics, no feelings whatsoever as he hacked at Alaisdair and breathed his foul green contagion into the air where they fought. Despite Alaisdair's leathers, the giant found a way to draw his blood. Though she desperately tried, she couldn't tear her eyes away, cringing as Alaisdair slipped in his own gore, the giant finishing him as he tried to catch himself on the way down. When the giant stood up, he held Alaisdair's head in his free hand as he waved his sword and shouted in triumph. The giant looked exactly like the monster Tristan had defeated all those centuries ago. At the sight of Alaisdair's handsome face contorted in pain, his hair in the monster's grip, her world went black.

From the corner of his eye, Alaisdair saw Shanley collapse onto the cold stone floor. Dropping his claymore, he ran to scoop her up and cradle her in his arms. As he held her, he felt the hot wetness of her tears bathing his chest, and he panicked at her pain.

Scathach's pleased expression as she joined them sent shivers down his spine. "So that's the way of it. Two Conlan prophetesses, one for each generation. The druid side of the Conlan clan runs deep even into the warriors, it seems."

Alaisdair glanced at the warrior goddess. "Ye were tryin' tae accelerate our bondin' with the strenuous trainin', were ye, milady?"

With her hands on her hips, a subtle red and gold aura pulsing around her, she left no doubt of her displeasure at his thinly disguised censure. "It is necessary. We have not much time as you know."

Shanley was a prophetess. It was her job to let him know what the future might hold for him, allowing him a chance to prepare. Speaking quietly for Shanley's ears only, Alaisdair coaxed her from her trance. "Lass, I wish yer visions weren't so terrible they cause ye tae pass out." He planted a kiss on her mouth when she blinked open her eyes. "I'm still here with ye. I havnae crossed the ford with the Morrigan."

She groaned, drawing Scathach's attention.

"I know the vision exhausted you, Shanley, but we need to know what you saw."

Shanley stared up at Alaisdair, fear and confusion in her eyes. Tentatively, she ran her fingers over his face.

"Ye've had a prophecy, lass. Like yer niece, ye're a prophetess. I know 'twas a painful thing ye experienced, but ye must tell us what ye saw." He stroked his hand over her hair and kissed her forehead. "Please, Shan."

Gulping back tears, she related her vision in a thready voice.

"You're set upon by three rogue warriors. Then the Morhaus sickens you with the green contagion of his breath before he attacks. You fight him valiantly, but he takes advantage of your weakened state. He hacks through your leathers. When you slip in your own blood, he takes a two-handed swing of his claymore and, and—" Tears replaced words.

Guessing the end but knowing he needed to hear it all, Alaisdair whispered into her ear. "Finish it, lass."

The pain in her eyes undid him, but the fact she trusted him enough to let him see it elated him. No doubt, theirs would be a long, happy, and intimate relationship—if they survived Samhain.

Shuddering in a breath, she sniffed back her tears. "He s-separates your head from your body. Then he p-picks up your head by the hair and holds it high in victory. Morgan watches with a smug grin before she turns in triumph to stare me down with her glowing red eyes."

She turned her tear-wet face into his chest and wept silently while he smoothed his hands up and down her back. "Shh, lass, 'tis all right. I'm here, safe and sound. Ye're only seein' what *could* happen if we aren't prepared, not what *will* happen. Remember that."

As she finished retelling her vision, the massive chamber resonated with the desperate silence of people not willing to breathe in dread of giving the prophecy life.

With her usual no-nonsense efficiency, Scathach scanned her warrior band and spoke over the fear and grief Shanley's prophecy generated. "In your prophcy, do you see why Alaisdair is outside his cottage alone?"

"A little compassion, milady?" Rio asked. "Shanley just watched Alaisdair die."

Even though he'd witnessed Rio's proclivity to challenge the goddess on several previous occasions, Alaisdair still couldn't believe how much the man dared. Right now, he was grateful as silent sobs rocked Shanley's body as he held her in his arms.

"Unfortunately, Rio, we do not have the time for compassion.

My sisters have some terrible plans for Alaisdair and for you, plans they intend to enact soon." Dismissing him with a nod, she returned her attention to Shanley. "Again, why is Alaisdair alone outside his cottage?"

Shanley shook her head in the negative.

"Hmm. Well, then, we will have to see if we can discover the answer."

Scathach turned her attention to Alaisdair. "Come, you must engage with the three Sheridan brothers. They will be the rogue warriors attacking you before the Morhaus arrives. We will determine what sorts of tactics you can employ should this scenario come to pass." She walked around the rest of the assembly until she stood before Owen. "While your sons train, continue your work with Ceri on her shield. Sian, work with Shanley. Alyssa and Lynnette, you will attempt to breach Ceri and Shanley's shields. We need to do as much as we can to help our prophetesses compartmentalize the present and the possible future in their minds."

The combination of sorrow and fear Alaisdair saw in Shanley's eyes ripped his heart out. Risking the goddess's wrath, he hugged her close and kissed her forehead. "We've both outwitted the unholy trio fer years, lass. We'll outwit them this time tae. Ye'll see."

He stood and helped Shanley to her feet. With his hand in the small of her back, he ushered her over to join Owen and the other talismans.

It was apparent Scathach had decided to give him his tiny moment of rebellion. Instead of chastising them for not jumping to her commands, she merely continued her instruction. "As you work with Sian, I will train you to be both in the prophecy and outside it simultaneously. Normally, it takes years of training to be able to master the skill of compartmentalizing your mind to experience the prophecy while also remaining in the present moment, but we do not have that kind of time. At best, we have two days."

Shanley flinched back into Alaisdair's hand on the small of her back while Scathach went on, seemingly oblivious to the impact of her predictions. "At worst, we have this afternoon and evening. Either way, we need to start now."

Shanley sucked in air, turned, and gifted Alaisdair with a wan smile. Understanding he'd been dismissed, he retrieved his claymore and backed his way over to rejoin the rest of the warriors, his eyes never leaving his talisman.

"You have had premonitions of Alaisdair in battles with three of Morgan's rogue warriors, correct?"

Shanley nodded.

"Where do these battles take place?"

She blinked, a look of surprise flitting across her face at Scathach's lack of emotion. Even though he'd been training with the goddess regularly since Rio Sheridan arrived at Conlan Manor, Alaisdair still hadn't become accustomed to Scathach's abrupt nature. He couldn't blame Shanley for her responses, yet his heart swelled with pride as he watched her straighten her spine, ready to take on whatever was coming.

She cleared her throat and said, "I may only have met him two days ago, but I've seen Alaisdair in premonitions and waking dreams for years, which makes retelling them nauseating. I'm sorry, milady." She shut her eyes tight, squared her shoulders, and told the goddess what she wanted to know, stealing Alaisdair's heart in the process.

It was rather unnerving to hear one's death described in such lurid detail, yet he could see his discomfort was nothing compared to the pain Shanley endured in the retelling of her prophecy. Before he had time to process her revelations, Scathach launched an attack on the warrior band, and their training resumed on the instant whim of the warrior goddess.

As the family trained, Scathach casually walked around the training room, first observing the attack on Alaisdair and coaching him on how to move and when to use the tactics she'd insisted he practice with Rio in earlier training sessions. Then she turned her attention to the shielding training with the talismans. As the day wore on with no additional prophecies, she called a break. Sweat poured off warriors and talismans alike, and though everyone had been working at their capacity, Scathach was not pleased.

She paced impatiently as the band drank deeply of the water Hamish had so thoughtfully supplied. "Shanley's premonitions and her vision are connected to the prophecies Ceri had of Rio taking on the Morhaus in the clearing beside Alaisdair's cottage. That much is clear."

The warriors knew of Ceri's prophecies. Like her aunt, she'd experienced the first one in the training room, brought on by Scathach's intense attacks on Rio during a training session. Alaisdair and the Sheridans had witnessed Ceri's other vision in the salon at Conlan Manor, which terrified them as they watched her lose all contact with time and reality.

Alaisdair admitted to himself how much he worried for his own talisman's sanity as she confronted the powers of her special skill. He slid a glance at Shanley as he downed a liter of icy water.

"We must find a way to discover how Morgan will try to lure both Rio and Alaisdair out onto the open grounds of the manor." Scathach paced away from the knot of warriors and talismans gathered around the cooler of bottled water and snacks of fruit, nuts, and protein bars.

To cool himself down, Alaisdair poured frigid water over his head and chest.

It seemed the warriors and talismans barely rested before Scathach put them through their paces again. After another hour of intense training, everyone except the goddess dripped sweat. Warriors and talismans alike labored to draw breath, yet Scathach growled with irritation.

Standing in the middle of the stone floor and tapping her

foot, she said, "I thought the additional training might bring about another prophecy."

Inside his mind, Alaisdair sighed. After the second round of training, he'd started to think maybe he wouldn't have the stamina to take care of the other, equally important part of bonding with his talisman. Yes, they'd needed to discover her skill, an event which the training had accelerated. Still, the more pleasurable private pursuits of a warrior with his talisman were necessary for making them a strong fighting unit too. It seemed Scathach believed their battle training superceded all else.

Catching his thoughts, Shanley stared at him with alarm, a bottle of water halfway to her lips. Alaisdair grinned at her and quirked a brow.

"Donnae worry, lass. It'll take more than a single-minded goddess tae slow me down when it comes tae bondin' with ye."

Shanley's eyebrows nearly touched her hairline before she smiled a secret little smile just for him. *"Good to know, warrior."*

He doubled over with his hands on his knees, laboring to draw in breath, when he picked up Rio's unshielded thoughts.

"Do you think you could leave us one scrap of energy to take care of our talismans when we're done here, milady?"

Alaisdair turned his head to stare at Rio in disbelief at the spiteful tone of his unguarded thoughts.

Scathach ignored her warriors' complaints. "Ceri's and Shanley's responses to their prophecies and dreams satisfies me that the two of you have done a remarkable job of bonding your talismans to you in so short a time." She paced a circle around the two warriors. "As the quintessential warrior of the age, Rio, no woman the fates had chosen for you could ever resist you. Then there are Shanley's dreams in which she has been steadily emotionally bonding with you, Alaisdair, for years. So, battle training remains the foremost activity in which you need to engage."

Huh. His thoughts hadn't been all that private. At least he

wasn't alone in them. Somehow, knowing Rio shared his frustrations brought the two of them closer. Slow grins crossed their faces in simultaneous agreement. No matter how exhausted Scathach's training left them, they *would* take care of their talismans when they returned to Conlan Manor.

CHAPTER FIFTEEN

OR THE REST of the day, Scathach ran the warriors through various scenarios. Though she couldn't conjure weather like her brother god Taranis, she did use light and sound to simulate some of Taranis's more common tactics. She wished she could call the mists, however, since she believed thick fog would be his tactic for Samhain. Morgan might be able to force Taranis to interfere with weather, but she couldn't tell him what weather to call.

Scathach remembered a long-ago battle the great Irish hero Brian Boru had won because Taranis, purely to spite Morgan for badgering him, called a mist rather than the ruinous thunderstorm Morgan had demanded. The mist more effectively shielded Brian Boru than his opponent whom Morgan had slated to best him. Scathach smiled at the remembered pleasure of Boru's triumph, and consequently her own triumph as his warrior goddess. Retaining the life of so heroic a warrior in the face of her sister's insatiable desire for warrior deaths had been singularly satisfying.

However, she faced a more pressing problem with her current champions. No doubt, Morgan remembered that battle with Brian Boru as well and wouldn't push Taranis for specific weather. Which would leave the choice up to Taranis and whatever mischief he chose that would be enough to give Morgan reason to leave him alone for a while. A god as unpredictable as Taranis presented Scathach with far too many scenarios.

"You appear deep in thought, milady. Is there anythin' ye need? Any way I can contribute tae yer trainin' these lads and lasses?"

"Hamish, did you invite my sister to your Samhain celebrations this year as usual?"

A sheepish expression crossed his face. "Milady, it seems a bit like tauntin', but I decided no' tae invite the Morrigan tae the festivities this year."

"Morgan can take that however she chooses—and she will. You have made a wise decision." She nodded to him with approval as she continued to watch her warriors practice. "What about Taranis?"

"The people in this part o' Scotland require his autumn storms fer gatherin' food from the sea, as ye know."

"Perhaps your invitation will be enough incentive for him to limit his weather shenanigans at Conlan Manor to light mists."

"We can only hope." Hamish smiled at her. "The locals who attend the ceilidh enjoy a good wander about the grounds at midnight as the ladies prepare the supper. A mist is just the thing fer givin' 'em a little Samhain atmosphere."

Scathach stared at the intricate Celtic knot carvings in the ceiling of the chamber and silently berated herself. While she worked her warriors to exhaustion in the attempt to elicit a prophecy out of one or the other of the newly discovered prophetesses, the answer to her question was plain. Hamish Buchanan's Samhain celebrations always included a foray around the grounds of Conlan Manor. The civilians saw it as a lark to scare away "evil spirits" while the warriors understood their obligations to the world beyond the mists, making sure the ancestors and the gods were given their due in a ritual trek over the grounds.

During this moment, no doubt, Morgan would strike, sending her rogue warriors and zombie champions against Scathach's hastily trained warrior band. The ritual sealing of the grounds of the estate would be the reason for Alaisdair and Rio to be outside the manor in a vulnerable position to take whoever Morgan had up her sleeve to send against them. Taranis would almost have to send the mists to shield the civilians from witnessing the otherworldly battle sure to take place.

Telescoping her thoughts back into the present, she said to Hamish, "As usual, you have been quite helpful. I believe we are finished for today."

Signaling an end to the battle practice, Scathach commanded both prophetesses and their warriors to visualize themselves back to Conlan Manor while the rest of the warrior band faced a long hike down the mountain, a skiff ride across the loch, and a drive from Ullapool to the manor. As she glanced around at her tired warriors, she smiled her mischievous thoughts. At times like these, it was good to be a goddess. Leaving behind a red and gold shimmer in the air, Scathach bent time and space to return to her home on Tara in the heart of Ireland. She had more planning to do.

CHAPTER SIXTEEN

"WHAT SORT OF precautions?"

Hamish and Owen were enjoying a cup of tea in the kitchens following their return to Conlan Manor. The rest of the clan had disappeared into their various bedrooms. With half an ear, Alaisdair listened to the men talk while he prepared a tray of food to take to Shanley who awaited him in her room upstairs.

"Alaisdair has reinforced both Rio's and his leathers, and I've added extra enchantments tae the manor and the cottage. Rio has looked at the area where the fightin' might go on and knows where he must avoid allowin' the rogues tae lure him or force him tae move."

"Reinforced his leathers how?" Owen glanced over to Alaisdair working at the counter beside the fridge.

Looking away from the roast beef sandwiches he was preparing, Alaisdair said, "After Ceri's initial prophecy, I had the idea tae reinforce our jackets with lightweight mesh like ye see divers use when they think they might encounter sharks. I fashioned sleeves and slid them between the lining and the leather since Ceri prophesied Rio losing control of his sword arm during the battle." He arranged thick roast beef sandwiches on plates. "I also added an extra strip o' protection down the center o' the back." He glanced up from his task. "Makes the jackets a bit heavy, but still serviceable."

Owen grimaced. "Seems like we're reverting to the Middle Ages."

"We made these precautions before Shanley arrived and Alaisdair discovered her tae be his talisman. There may be differences now." Hamish's tone drew Alaisdair's attention. "That's the way o' it with prophecy. It's an inexact gift, but it does allow us tae plan rather than merely tae react."

"I think all of us should reinforce our leathers before we meet Morgan this time," Owen suggested.

"There's extra metal mesh on the worktable in Hamish's apartment. Help yerself," Alaisdair said as he picked up a tray laden with sandwiches and a pot of tea. "I have another obligation tae attend tae." He couldn't help the grin spreading across his face.

"A fine obligation she is, one ye deserve auld friend."

Owen smiled and saluted Alaisdair with his mug of tea.

As Alaisdair climbed the stairs, he thought he heard Owen ask how they were going to be able to build in all the security measures they needed in time for the ceilidh at Samhain. Alaisdair had wondered the same thing, but he had more pressing matters. Namely, the comfort of his talisman who, to his mind, had endured one hell of an afternoon.

When he shouldered open the door to Shanley's room, he discovered her staring out the windows at the front gardens. He closed the door with his heel and set the tray on the bureau.

Wrapping his arms around her and pulling her into his chest felt natural, like coming home. She sighed and covered his hands with hers. *We're like an auld married pair already,* he thought.

"Sort of jumping the gun there, aren't you warrior?"

"What?"

"We have to live through Samhain first, and then there might be one or two other obstacles to deal with—like an ocean and a continent separating our homes," she said dryly.

But she didn't move away from him.

"A discussion fer another time, lass. Right now, I've more pressin' things tae think about." He slid a hand down her belly and pulled her in tight, letting her know exactly what was on his mind, shield or no shield.

"Guess we're supposed to be open to each other. Isn't that what you said last night?" she teased, but the seriousness of her expression when she turned in his arms didn't match her tone.

Though he'd only known her a short time, he surprised himself with how well he could read her. "We'll figure out the logistics, Shan. But there is nae way I'll ever be separated from ye now that I've found ye."

He punctuated his resolve with a soft kiss, a brush of his lips over hers before he tightened his arms around her and intentionally overwhelmed her. The kiss flashed from zero to bonfire in the space of two heartbeats. Alaisdair ground his hard-on against her soft belly, and Shanley changed the game. Twining her left leg around him, she opened herself to him and kissed him back with all the heat he'd given her as she rubbed her hot center along his length. Before he knew it, he was the one gasping for air.

Determined to return to his plan for taking care of her, he walked her backward until the backs of her thighs hit the mattress. When she fell back, he tumbled down on top of her. Rolling to her side, he leaned up on one elbow, grinned down at her, and said, "As my talisman, ye get tae call the shots on the battlefield. But in this room, I'm goin' tae take charge."

Her eyes widened, and he cut off her protest with his lips and his hands. Peeling her sweater off, he followed his hands with his mouth, swirling his tongue in her bellybutton, enjoying the shivers playing over her skin as he licked and nipped his way up her taut torso to her bra.

"Alaisdair."

"Hmmm?"

"You're driving me wild."

When he glanced up at her over the mounds of her full breasts, he smiled at the dark desire he saw in the deep green forests of her eyes.

"Though I love the way ye look in this lacy white bra, I want my tongue on more o' yer beautiful skin."

"And a poet, too. Oooh."

Her moans told him she preferred skin-on-skin touching when he slipped his fingers beneath the band and pushed her bra over her head without bothering with the niceties of unclasping it first.

With his thumb and forefinger, he plucked and rolled the pebbled tightness of one rosy nipple while he drew the other deep into his mouth, sucking and lapping at her with his tongue. She buried her fingers in his hair, dislodging the leather string he'd used to tie it back and tugging enough to let him know how much she enjoyed his touch. Whimpering her pleasure, she held him to her when he transferred his feasting mouth to her other breast.

The pressure built behind the fly of his jeans as she arched and writhed beneath him. The responsiveness of his woman was as much an aphrodisiac as the satin of her skin, the beauty of her heavy breasts, nipped-in waist, and full hips. He wanted to touch and taste all of her, but her whimpers and moans said she wanted something else.

"This needs to come off *now*," she growled as she tugged at his sweater, catching his T-shirt on her way to divesting him of his clothes.

"Glad ye're in this as far as I am, lass." He chuckled as she flung his clothes to the floor beside the bed.

"You're not far enough in at *all*, warrior." She batted her eyes impishly at him. "But we can fix that directly."

He huffed out a laugh that ended in a groan. In seconds, her busy hands had unzipped his fly and were pushing at the waist-bands of his jeans and boxers.

Enjoying her eagerness, he reached down to help her when he caught a whiff of her scent. Musky, a hint of jasmine, a little sweat—all her. His nostrils flared, and he couldn't wait either. Time had barely ticked forward when their clothes lay in a tangled heap on the floor, their bodies tangled up in each other on the bed as he buried himself so deep inside her he forgot where he ended and she began.

CHAPTER SEVENTEEN

WHEN SHANLEY HAD agreed to fly to Scotland to help Ceri with the Samhain rituals Hamish said were required of them, she'd had no idea what she'd gotten herself into. This year's event had become so much bigger than the Samhain ceilidh she remembered from her year in the manor. Interspersed with the training sessions over the past few days had been Rio's frantic insistence on the Sheridans helping him to wire in as much of the security system as possible before All Hallows Eve. After all, installing the security system had been reason he'd traveled to Scotland in the first place. Both Hamish and Alaisdair continued to insist the security precautions weren't necessary. Still, Rio persisted.

The Samhain preparations themselves were yet another matter. The manor positively swarmed with an army of local civilians and druids as they spent the days leading to Samhain preparing food and decorating the massive ballroom on the third floor. As she stood in the middle of the front foyer on the afternoon of Samhain, activity pulsed through Shanley in waves. The kitchens were overrun with older women cooking up *neeps* and *tatties*, the turnips and mashed potatoes required for a proper ceilidh, along with the *haggis*, the sausage made of oats and sheep's innards boiled in a sheep's stomach. Smells wafting from the kitchens made her stomach growl. Though the haggis sounded like something no one would eat, Shanley knew from experience how delectable it was, especially when mixed altogether with neeps and tatties.

Davy Sutherland, Hamish's prized druid student and from what Shanley gathered, a source of some contention between Rio and Hamish, appeared to be chatting amiably with Hamish as they chanted over the rowan branches they hung over the front door. People raced up and down the stairs carrying armloads of tartan and more rowan branches and bouquets of autumn flowers in purple, goldenrod, maroon, and fiery orange. The activities buffeting her wore her out.

With a sigh, she retreated to the sitting room to the right of the front door. Though she desperately wanted to help with the decorating or the cooking or the chanting or something, she couldn't. During the previous day's training session, she and Ceri had simultaneously endured a prophecy so terrifying, even a day later she remained physically and emotionally drained from it. Thinking about what might come that evening sent shivers through her that had nothing to do with the crisp autumn air gently blowing through the open front door.

As she sank down onto the lumpy sofa, she absently picked at loose threads and stared out the windows facing the veranda at the front of the house. Yet she didn't see the autumn splendor of the front gardens, the source of those gorgeous flowers carried upstairs earlier. Instead, she saw Alaisdair and Hamish, Finn and Rio, battling rogue warriors and the ancient zombies Morgan reanimated for tonight's battle. She and Ceri enduring the same vision simultaneously had even rattled Scathach. If Morgan did indeed strike during the ceilidh, Shanley didn't think she'd ever want to attend another.

"There ye are, Shan."

"Alaisdair! You scared the hell out of me!"

Lost in her thoughts, she hadn't noticed him until he gently rubbed her thigh and spoke softly to her. When she jumped, he held her down with his hands on the tops of her thighs.

"Ye were in yer own little world. At first when I called tae ye and ye dinnae answer, I worried ye were havin' another prophecy. But yer eyes look different when that's happenin'." He sat on the couch beside her, slid his arm over her shoulders and pulled her into his side. "This time, ye were far away of yer own will. Want tae talk about it?"

She side-eyed him. "You didn't help yourself to my thoughts already?"

"Since yer first vision, yer shield is rather formidable, did ye know that?"

With a sigh, she settled into him. "I trust you. Implicitly. Completely. You believe me, right?"

"I dae, lass. Yeah. I wasnae accusin' ye. I thought I might be able tae have a look around in yer thoughts since ye weren't respondin' tae my voice."

"Maybe that only works after we've been together for longer than a few days."

"Reckon we'll have tae test yer theory," he said with a smile before he leaned in and brushed his lips lightly over her temple.

"If we get the chance."

She thought she sounded normal, but the way Alaisdair looked at her when he pulled back said otherwise.

"So that's the way o' it. Ye've been sittin' here stewin' about taenight and what might not even happen when the veil between this world and the next is at its thinnest."

Unable to deny it, she nodded.

With supernatural warrior speed and strength, Alaisdair hauled Shanley up to straddle his lap before she gasped her next breath.

"Alaisdair!"

There was no playful grin on his mouth when he cupped her face in his big, calloused hands and stared deeply into her eyes. "Ye've given me so much already. Not the least of which is a strategy fer combating the Morhaus if that's who Morgan sends against me. Ye gave Scathach insights intae how her sister plans tae try tae take us. We've trained fer scenarios none of us could have imagined on our own." He pulled her forehead down to touch his. "We're a strong team, ye and I. When this is all over, we'll be even stronger." He rubbed his bearded cheek along hers. "After all these years alone, there's nae way I'm crossin' the ford fer Morgan's pleasure taenight." He brushed a soft kiss over her mouth. "When this evenin' ends, I'll be in yer bed with ye, and we'll be makin' plans fer our future."

"You seem so sure."

"Because I've seen it, Shanley."

Jerking back, she felt her eyes round as she stared at him. "You're a prophet as well as a warrior?"

"Nae, lass. Naethin' so exotic as all that. But I've dreamed of my talisman tae."

Her hand flew to her mouth when he grinned at her gaping at him.

"In my dreams, I'm with my mate. I cannae see her face, but I can feel her devotion tae me—tae us—and tae our fated union. Always, my talisman holds me in her heart, and I keep her safe in mine. That's what gives me courage tae face whatever we're goin' tae face, Shan." He wrapped her in his arms and pulled her flush against his chest. "We both felt the electric charge melding us tae-gether even before I tried my sign on ye. Knowin' I have ye beside me tells me I dreamed true."

She buried her face in the crook of his neck and returned his fierce embrace. Somewhere, a grandfather clock chimed the hour—five bells.

Hamish poked his head through the door to the sitting room, interrupting their quiet moment. As one, they gave their attention to him.

"It's time tae ready ourselves fer the evenin'. I've sent the civilians on their way with a promise tae start the festivities at eight o'clock sharp."

Shanley returned her face to Alaisdair's neck, inhaling the scent of the forest on his skin deep into her lungs. Breathing this man inside her might be her only way of hanging onto him.

"Thanks, Hamish. We'll join ye fer dinner in a few minutes."

Alaisdair rubbed his bearded cheek over Shanley's hair. "Ye havnae been listenin'. Lass, ye're no' goin' tae lose me taenight. Although breathing me inside ye sounds rather nice."

She felt as much as heard his chuckle before he moved against her, alerting her to his aroused state. Pulling away enough to see his face, she demanded, "How can you be thinking about that when the whole world might end tonight?"

"At this precise moment, my beautiful woman is straddling my lap with certain delicious and"—he flexed his hips, the hard front of his jeans rubbing her soft center—"rather heated parts of her snuggled up tight tae a certain hard part of me. What else could I be thinkin'?"

She couldn't stop the giggle bubbling out of her mouth. "You're incorrigible."

"That means sexy, right?"

"And I think I'm a little bit crazy about you."

The wicked smile on his face told her how much her revelation pleased him, negating the need for a foray into his thoughts. Because she couldn't help it, she leaned down and kissed him. She meant it to be a promise, but that smile should have warned her Alaisdair had other ideas.

Sometime not long enough later, Shanley heard a not-so-discreet cough.

"Hamish wants to know if the two of you are coming—" Ceri announced from the door of the sitting room—"to dinner," she finished with a chuckle.

Alaisdair pushed himself up from where he'd been lying in the space Shanley had made for him between her jean-clad thighs as he pleasured both of them with his attention to her naked breasts. Her face heated at being caught partially naked, and she tried to melt into the cushions.

"We'll be there in a minute."

How could he sound so calm after winding her up the way he'd been doing for the last however long?

Ceri's laughter echoed through the front foyer as she returned to the dining room. Shanley hastily tugged her sweater back over herself while Alaisdair threw himself back against the cushions of the sofa and huffed out a long-suffering sigh.

The sizzling desire that pulsed in his whisky-colored eyes as he watched her right herself nearly evaporated her resolve. But she knew better. As much as she'd rather finish what they'd started, they needed fuel for the coming battle. She didn't think the Sheridans would leave much for leftovers if she and Alaisdair didn't hustle themselves to the dining room for dinner.

Chapter Eighteen

SHANLEY COULDN'T HELP but enjoy herself with the Celtic fiddle music and the dancing of the reels during the Samhain ceilidh. The ballroom was a beacon of merriment, its lights spilling from the third story down the front of the manor. The Conlan plaid festooned the backs of chairs and covered the round tables edging the central dance floor. Artfully arranged bouquets of purple and rust hydrangeas, fiery autumn ivy, coral-colored begonias, and purple thistles centered the tables. Rowan branches guarded the windows and doors against evil spirits. While she appreciated the druidic care and symbolism the decorations represented, Shanley mostly enjoyed the people.

Everywhere she looked, local civilians as well as warriors, talismans, and druids sampled Hamish's mead and whisky and enjoyed lively conversation and laughter. The dance floor whirled with kilts and skirts of the local clans, a riot of colors and plaids.

Yet, as the ceilidh neared its climax at the midnight hour, she couldn't tamp down her rising nerves. Something ominous lurked beyond the party. Judging from the tense lines bracketing her niece's pretty mouth, Ceri felt it too.

Though Ceri and Shanley had dressed in the lavender, meadow green, and heather plaid of the Conlans and Alyssa, Sian, and Lynnette wore the forest green, azure blue, and tan plaids of the Sheridans, their festive attire couldn't hide their trepidation for what they sensed Morgan planned to unleash on their warriors. Hamish only intensified Shanley's worry when he stepped up to the dais in front of the band.

"Lads, it's come tae the witchin' hour. Time tae take our traditional tour o' the grounds tae ward off the evil spirits," he said with a chuckle. "With Saraid's expert supervision"—he nodded at the old druid woman standing below the dais—"the women will set out the midnight supper."

A cheer went up from the civilian men who saw this part of the evening as a lark, an excuse to wander the grounds, drink whisky, and tell bawdy stories out of earshot of the ladies. Shanley knew full well Hamish's announcement was the cue for the assembled warriors to take on Morgan and her unholy army in a parallel time and place veiled by mists. After all, Shanley had been watching this particular show rather regularly in premonitions for years.

On her first visit to Conlan Manor, Hamish had introduced her to Saraid, one of his trusted friends. At Hamish's pronouncement, Saraid sent the talismans and druid women to the kitchens. The talismans knew to make it look like they were joining the others, but Hamish had instructed them to disappear into his apartments. If Morgan attempted an attack on the manor, the talismans would be safe there. Knowing she had no other choice, Shanley followed the others downstairs and wished again she was a dreamer rather than a prophetess. Like generals in battle, dreamers like the Sheridan women could watch and direct their warriors in real time.

Prophetesses like Ceri and her could only hope their

prophecies had prepared their warriors well enough to avoid the fates those prophecies predicted.

Shanley gravitated to Ceri, clasping her hand and holding on tight. Deep in her mind, she wished her first battle in her role as Alaisdair's talisman were something less dire than the fate of the Conlan clan. Ceri smiled wanly at her as the women entered Hamish's apartment and settled in to wait.

Alaisdair and Hamish came upon the Morhaus near Alaisdair's cottage exactly as Shanley had seen. Though he thought he'd prepared for Morgan's mythical champion, the reality of the beast proved infinitely more terrible. Insensible to the rogue warriors Morgan sent with it to take on the Sheridans, the monster left several of them dead or dying near it, victims of its rancid breath.

Wisely, Hamish brought with him large handkerchiefs over which he'd applied a thin layer of nightshade salve before he'd handed them out to the warriors accompanying him. When they saw the sulfurous fog surrounding the Morhaus, every warrior tied on his bandana to shield himself from the beast's most powerful weapon.

The local warriors Hamish had invited to the ceilidh spread out and took on the rogues who looked to please the Morrigan by being the one to give her the prize of Alaisdair Graham skewered on the blade of a claymore. Alaisdair tried to keep Hamish in his sights as he took on first one then two rogue warriors who materialized out of the mists.

Civilians with torches in a parallel dimension walked the perimeter of the manor grounds, oblivious to the fighting raging beside them. Their flashlights cast a feeble light on the battle, giving Alaisdair scant help. His fellow warriors took on rogues who fought like a pack of wolves, ganging up together on one seemingly vulnerable prey.

Since Shanley had warned him to expect this assault, he was more prepared than the rogues suspected. He feinted toward one, pretending not to notice the second. In one smooth motion, he spun on his toes, a lithe dancer in a macabre ballet, tilted his claymore, and filleted the second rogue from his pubis to his Adam's apple. The momentum from his well-timed blow carried him around to engage the other's sword as the rogue moved to strike a killing blow to the back of Alaisdair's head. The shock of the claymores coming together knocked the rogue's sword from his hand, and Alaisdair finished him with a sharp in-and-out stab to the front of his neck, piercing his windpipe and severing his spine. The man dropped to the ground in a puddle of his own blood.

Leaving him no time to appreciate his success, two more rogues walked out of the mists, calmly stepping over their fallen comrades to engage him head-on. *These at least showed some honor coming at me face-to-face*, Alaisdair thought fleetingly before the two rushed him at once. He surely would have gone down had Rowan Sheridan not appeared at his side at that precise moment, crouching and swinging his claymore to trip one of their opponents with a well-timed blow at his ankles while the other glanced a blow off the shoulder of Alaisdair's reinforced leathers. The shot to his shoulder momentarily stunned him before he regained his composure and faced his next partner in Morgan's deadly dance.

Alaisdair and Rowan fought a seemingly never-ending onslaught of rogue warriors before the Morhaus reemerged from the mists. It appeared the monster had waited and watched as the two heroes took on his mistress's army. The monster must have thought Alaisdair and Rowan looked weakened enough to attack. Waving his huge bull's head around, he bellowed out his putrid breath.

The warriors' treated handkerchiefs had slipped from their faces during their battles with the rogues, and they scrambled to reapply them before the foul air emanating from the Morhaus overcame them, a tactic the monster hadn't anticipated. It also hadn't anticipated Hamish's chanting from somewhere behind it. Hamish's Gaelic song enervated the Morhaus, making its movements sluggish and uncoordinated.

It seemed Rowan didn't speak Gaelic, so he suffered no ill effects from Hamish's efforts. On the other hand, Alaisdair needed to avoid succumbing to Hamish's chant as well. He opened his shield and called to Shanley. *"Lass, I need yer help. Remind me how I defeat the Morhaus."*

Even via telepathy, Alaisdair caught Shanley's gasp of relief when he reached out to her. *"He's going to subdue you with his breath. Stay away from the front of his face. Feint from side to side, get his head lolling back and forth before you step close to reach behind his thigh to hamstring him with your claymore. Use the tricky maneuver you practiced with Rio."*

Shanley's directions took Alaisdair's mind off Hamish's hypnotizing chants. As she had directed, he executed a spin and a feint, allowing him to slip behind the giant and slice him deeply through the backs of both his legs. As the monster buckled under his own weight, he roared in pain and swung his massive arms, trying to catch whatever he could in his wide angry arc.

He caught Alaisdair in his midsection on a backswing, sending him flying. The hard landing on the edge of the hill winded him, and he lay still. The Morhaus tried to finish him, but his legs were useless. With the monster distracted in his search for Alaisdair, Rowan stepped in and executed a mighty blow, partially decapitating the beast. The giant's eyes rolled in his head, and Rowan finished him off with a second powerful swing of his claymore.

"Thank you, friend," Alaisdair panted when he could finally draw air back into his lungs. The painful fire that masqueraded as breathing told him the Morhaus had probably broken a few of his ribs, but the monster hadn't succeeded in killing him.

"You're welcome. Thank you for making it easy for me. You've perfected that special move Scathach taught Rio," Rowan replied, appreciation in his tone before his face took on a look of concern. "Are you hurt? Can you stand?"

"I think the beast broke some o' my ribs with that last blow. Ye all right?"

"Scratches and bruises. Come on, let's find a safe place for you to rest, somewhere where we can protect you from rogue stragglers who'd take advantage of a wounded man," Rowan said as he helped Alaisdair to his feet.

"We're near my cottage. It's heavily enchanted. Take me there and then go help the others. Have ye seen Rio?"

"No, and I'm worried. Riley and my dad were fighting with Finn near Hamish, keeping him safe as Scathach instructed. Somewhere, Rio got separated, and I can't penetrate his shield to know where or how he is. Now is not the time for him to be stubborn or heroic." Rowan's exasperation—and care for his younger brother—came through loud and clear in the growl of his voice. He slid an arm around Alaisdair when he staggered and asked, "How far to your cottage? I can't see much of anything in this fog. Can't help thinking it's just for us."

"We're used tae Taranis's fog around here. He sends it often." Alaisdair labored for breath. "My cottage is probably a hundred meters tae yer left. I can feel it," he said through sips of air.

"You're in worse shape than you're letting on. We need to hide you for a while."

⟡

Owen Sheridan found Alaisdair lying on his bed in the cottage clad in nothing but his jeans and socks, the extent of his injuries obvious in the blue and purple bruises decorating his naked torso. Though she'd been told to remain in the manor, Shanley hadn't obeyed once she figured out Alaisdair had been hurt. She

was measuring strips of bandages to wrap Alaisdair's ribs and fuss-
ing over him when Owen unceremoniously interrupted them. "I
need ropes and something to fashion a sling—a blanket will do,"
he said without explanation.

Shanley gasped, pain twisting her beautiful features. "Ceri's
prophecy came true. Oh, dear Lord. Does she know?"

"Her prophecy is only partly true. Rio's alive, but we need to
rescue him, and we don't have time to waste." The edge in Owen's
tone propelled Alaisdair off the bed.

He tried to breathe and move simultaneously, grimacing
when stabbing pain lanced through his ribs, but his friend's life
was at stake, so his battle wasn't over. "Hand me a clean shirt,
Shan," he said as he gritted his teeth and bent to pull on his boots.

"You're in no shape to go back out there, Alaisdair Graham."

"I've experienced worse. Hand me a shirt, please," he said,
making sure she heard his resolve. Owen nodded his approval as
he awaited Alaisdair. "There's a blanket in the closet in the hallway.
We'll have tae send tae Hamish's apartments fer rope."

As he gingerly shrugged back into his reinforced leather jacket,
he said, "Lass, ye know this is our lot. When we best the auld girl
by rescuin' Rio, it'll all be worth it." His short speech winded him,
and he sipped air before continuing. "Now get yer pretty self over
here and give me some incentive fer rejoinin' the fray."

Judging from the worry etched into her beautiful features,
his attempt at levity hadn't worked. Still, she stepped over to him
and gently wrapped her arms around his neck. To him, their kiss
tasted of promise. He hoped she felt it too.

⋘

Shanley wrung her hands and worried about how Alaisdair
thought he'd fend off rogue warriors or help lift Rio up from
the bottom of the ravine with broken ribs. His pain was enough
to send her to her knees though she hid her connection to him

behind a façade of efficiency and nagging. Sure, warriors possessed supernatural healing powers, but they were still human, still mortal. Judging from the way he moved, like he was trying not to breathe, Alaisdair's injuries were far more serious than he wanted anyone—especially her—to know.

"He'll come back to you, Shanley. Don't worry. He's a warrior. No doubt he's suffered worse as he's skirted Morgan all these years. Have faith in him," Sian Sheridan said, trying to reassure her.

Sian had joined Shanley in the cottage when Owen summoned her to bring rope from Hamish's apartment. Alyssa followed close behind, even though all of them defied Hamish—and Scathach—by not remaining safe inside the manor.

Shanley stared at the open door through which Alaisdair had left. "How do you do it Sian? How do you send Owen out the door so easily and with such confidence?" She didn't attempt to hide her tears.

"It's the only way I can survive being married to a warrior."

As they spoke, a blur resembling Ceri sped out the front door of the cottage before they could stop her. Running after Ceri, Lynnette called out over her shoulder, "Ceri can't get through to Rio. She's frantic, but I'll bring her back."

Shanley took a step toward the door, but Sian stayed her with a hand on her forearm. "It's not safe out there. You know that. Ceri has made herself a liability. Don't do the same."

"It's your entire family out there. How can you be so stoic?" Shanley cried before she saw the tears shimmering in Sian's eyes.

"We do our jobs. It isn't a choice if we're putting our warriors first."

The sadness in her tone nearly broke Shanley's heart, but she allowed Sian to pull her farther back into the cottage. Together, they sat in the middle of the couch in front of Alaisdair's fireplace, clasping each other's hand tightly, as they awaited the outcome of the battle.

꧁

At the top of the hill, five warriors worked to pull Rio Sheridan and his brothers from the ravine into which he'd fallen. Sweat poured from the men, but none of them broke their rhythm or gave in to fatigue. Alaisdair's torso was on fire, but he gritted his teeth against the pain and pulled on the rope with all the strength he had left.

Ceri's prophecy had mostly come true. Rio Sheridan had taken on the Welsh zombie giant *Ysbaddaden*, killed him—again—but in the process, he'd tumbled down the rocky ravine. Yet, it seemed the man lived. His brothers, Riley and Rowan, had fashioned a litter from the blanket and loaded Rio's inert form into it. Now Alaisdair, Owen, and several local warriors pulled on the rope attached to the brothers to help them out of the ravine.

He could hear Scathach encouraging them to hurry while high overhead, Morgan's ravens circled and mocked their efforts.

Encouraging him against his pain, Shanley communicated telepathically with Alaisdair, and he clung to her words even more tightly than he clung to the rope in his hands. *"I've known you in my dreams. You are the strongest warrior and greatest protector of Conlan Manor. Concentrate on your power. Draw on your power."*

With one last heave, the Sheridan brothers topped the rim of the ravine. When his brothers set him down, Rio blinked his eyes open and boiled up off the makeshift litter, wild and spoiling for a fight. Riley, who still held Rio's claymore after retrieving it from the ravine, jerked forward as Rio summoned his sword back to himself. Before the team could shout in victory and relief at Rio's apparent recovery, an army of rogue warriors set upon them.

On the balls of their feet, Alaisdair, the Sheridans, and their allies readied for battle, yet their claymores never tasted the flesh of the rogues who attacked them. Instead, they watched in amazement as first one then two and finally the rest rushed at them only to be rebuffed by an invisible wall—invisible that is until a rogue made contact with it. Then it lit up in a crackling storm of red and gold electricity like untamed lightning. Every rogue who contacted it died in a quivering jelly of flesh on the ground before it until at last, those in the rear of the attack wised up and slunk away into the mists.

As they watched the fireworks from inside their protective shell, the warriors marveled at the awesome power of their patron goddess and nodded to each other, exchanging looks of incredulity and relief. Not understanding how Scathach's protective shield worked, the men kept their claymores at the ready and continued their slow walk to the cottage, surrounding Rio whose expression wavered between thunderous and murderous.

When they crossed the line into the enchanted perimeter of Alaisdair's cottage, Scathach lifted their shield. Noting the knot of people in front of the cottage, the men exchanged fearful glances. The situation was bad, but not in the way they expected. The old warrior, Finn Daly, lay on the slate walk with a gaping wound in his chest.

"Och, that's a bad one." Hamish said as he took over for the women trying to stanch Finn's blood. "We need tae take Finn tae my chambers where I have the proper tools and medicines tae help him."

Catching sight of him, Shanley ran to Alaisdair, ducking beneath his arm to help him into the cottage.

Hamish continued to give out orders. "Owen, Riley, Rowan, between the three o' ye, ye should be able tae carry Finn down the tunnel tae the manor. And sharp-like. Alyssa, lass, ye can assist me, as can ye Sian, but Ceri and Shanley, ye have yer warriors tae tend tae.

"Donnae be long takin' care o' yer business. We still have a ceilidh tae manage and a ritual tae complete," he warned.

With those directions, Hamish led the way through the cottage and down the tunnel to the manor. Everyone but Alaisdair and Shanley followed behind him, Ceri and Rio bringing up the rear in silence.

CHAPTER NINETEEN

NCE THE OTHERS left the cottage, Shanley attended to Alaisdair who seemed to deflate, sagging into her embrace.

"All right, Superman, let's get you to bed."

He nodded, and she staggered as she took more of his weight.

"You're too big for me to carry," she said only half-jokingly. "It's only a few steps, and you're going to have to help me by taking them."

A voice from the door of the cottage stopped them midstep.

"You *had* to come to Scotland, didn't you Shanley?"

Shanley stared at the man standing in the doorway to the cottage. "Logan? What are you doing here?"

Beside her, Alaisdair stiffened. "How dae ye know this rogue, lass?"

"Logan? He's a civilian. A colleague at my school," she said with an uneasy laugh.

Logan couldn't be a rogue, could he?

A terrible smile stretched his lips as Logan Malo's eyes glowed red. It had been years since she'd seen that expression.

Memory overwhelmed her as she remembered a much younger man standing in the middle of a country lane, blocking her way home to the manor.

"I see ye finally remember me." He took a step into the room.

"H-how did you survive this long?"

"Struck a deal with a goddess, o' course." His ugly grin turned feral as his accent switched from American to Scots. "If only ye would ha' kissed me. Just once."

She gasped.

"But I'll have the reward Morgan promised me years ago and again when she sent me tae America." He turned his attention to Alaisdair whose weight still rested heavily across Shanley's shoulders. "Like Tristan centuries ago, ye killed the Morhaus. And like Tristan, ye'll die with yer lady lookin' on. A fittin' end, I suspect."

"I'm sorry, Alaisdair. I didn't see this," Shanley cried.

"'Tis all right, Shan. None o' this is yer fault. Logan Malo and I go way back." He nodded at the other man. "I should have killed ye when ye turned rogue before ye even reached yer twenty-eighth birthday."

"Ye were always soft, Alaisdair Graham. After the beatin' the Morhaus gave ye, this will be easy."

Shanley gasped as Alaisdair disappeared from her side and reappeared behind Logan in the space of one labored breath. From the way Logan's eyes rounded, Shanley guessed he felt the tip of Alaisdair's sword somewhere in the middle of his back.

"We'll dae this outside, if ye donnae mind."

Logan leered at her. "Get ready tae have a real man, Shanley." He spun around to face Alaisdair.

The clash of steel on steel assaulted Shanley's ears, and she clamped her hands over them before she called out for help. *"Alaisdair is under attack. One more rogue was lying in wait for him. He needs help. He's too hurt to take him on alone."*

She had no idea if anyone heard her. In her panicked state,

she hadn't targeted any one person in the manor. The thought of losing Alaisdair when they'd come so close to beating Morgan this time terrified her to her soul.

Beneath the deadly sword song, she heard the grunts of men laboring to kill each other. What she didn't hear was the sound of aid coming from the manor. Stepping outside the cottage door, she stifled a scream as she watched the mesmerizing speed of the warriors' swords clashing against each other. From the way Alaisdair was retreating under Logan's onslaught, she knew he was weakening. Looking around for a way to assist her warrior, she spied some loose gravel beside the flagstone patio in front of the cottage. Surreptitiously squatting down, she grabbed a handful and waited. When Logan side-stepped Alaisdair's blow, she tossed pebbles at Logan's feet. Scrabbling to maintain his balance, he momentarily took his eyes off Alaisdair's claymore. Alaisdair took advantage, executing the spinning move Scathach had demanded he perfect.

Logan cursed as he went down, his last angry words directed at Shanley.

∽

She'd closed the door on Logan Malo's lifeless body before taking on half of Alaisdair's weight as she eased him to his bedroom. When he collapsed facedown across his bed and didn't move, panic set in.

"Alaisdair! Wake up! Come on, warrior."

It was all she could do to roll the dead weight of him onto his back. If he still breathed, at least he wouldn't suffocate in the softness of his pillows. Laying her palm over his heart confirmed his life force still flowed through him. But his breathing was shallow, and he wouldn't wake up even when Shanley shook him and shouted at him.

Not being a healer, she had no idea how to help beyond

binding his chest, which she'd already done before he headed back into battle. She removed his boots, opened his leather jacket, and unzipped the fly of his jeans, hoping the lack of constrictions would allow him to breathe easier. When he still didn't respond, she gave in.

"I need help with Alaisdair. He won't wake up."

Hamish responded immediately. *"We've got our hands full with Finn, but I'll send Saraid along tae ye directly."* His somber tone terrified her. They couldn't lose Finn.

And what about Alaisdair? Had it only been two days since they'd finally found each other? In so short a time, she'd bonded to him completely. Her eyes never left his beautiful form lying so still on the pretty quilt he'd specially commissioned for his bed. She couldn't lose him now. She couldn't.

Slapping her hand over her mouth, she choked back a sob. A talisman's job required her to remain strong for her warrior, no matter what. Her mother had drilled that lesson into her from the time she could remember. But no one had ever told her how to be strong when the man she'd fallen in love with lay unresponsive in the middle of his king-sized bed.

As she lightly ran her hands over his chest, letting him know she was with him, she could admit her feelings. First in dreams and then in the days since they'd met, she'd fallen in love with Alaisdair Graham.

The bed sagged beneath her as she climbed onto it. Careful not to jostle him, Shanley knelt and smoothed her hands over his body. Starting with his head, she finger-combed his auburn hair, memorizing the silky texture of the long strands. Her palms lingered on the soft beard he kept neatly trimmed over his hollow cheeks and square jaw. Leaning down, she brushed kisses over his brows, eyelids, cheeks, and finally over his perfectly sculpted lips. When she lifted her head, she squeezed her eyes shut against the pain. Alaisdair hadn't even twitched at her touch.

"Alaisdair, wake up. I'm here. I need you." She sucked back a sob.

"That's the idea, lass. Touchin' and talkin' tae yer man is a good start."

On a gasp, Shanley pushed up off the bed.

"But those tears are no' doin' him a bit o' good," Saraid scolded.

Until Saraid mentioned tears, Shanley had had no sense of the rivers running down her face. Hastily, she dashed them away with the heels of her hands, but when her eyes returned to Alaisdair's still form, a keening cry joined the tears.

"Can you help him? Please, you have to help him."

Saraid quirked a brow before glancing briefly at her forearm where Shanley held on with both hands. "I can—if ye let me go and give me room."

Stepping aside, Shanley studied the druid healer as she studied her patient. Tilting her head this way and that, Saraid walked around the bed, her eyes never leaving Alaisdair. She chanted something in Gaelic and waited. Chanted again and waited. Still, he didn't move, didn't give any indication he remained in the world. When Shanley emitted a fearful sniffle, Saraid rebuked her with a look so condescending, she wanted to curl up and hide in the wardrobe.

Tapping a finger against her thin lips, Saraid seemed to reach a decision. Before Shanley could ask, Saraid dawdled past her. Torn between leaving Alaisdair alone and seeing what the old woman was about, Shanley followed her as far as the doorway to the bedroom.

Saraid disappeared around the corner into the kitchen, and Shanley thought maybe the druid planned to make a potion. A short time later, she returned to the room sipping a mug of tea.

"Saraid—"

Saraid lifted her hand in the universal signal for stop. Settling herself on the chair beside the bed, she serenely sipped her tea.

Shanley divided her gaze between her warrior and the druid, but Alaisdair's condition never changed. Pacing impatiently had no effect on either of them.

As the silence dragged, on, Shanley thought she might lose her mind. Finally, she stood in front of Saraid and demanded, "I asked for help. He's completely unresponsive and has been for the last hour."

Saraid nodded.

A terrible dread descended on her, and she dropped hard to the braided rug on the floor. "Are we..." She swallowed over the lump in her throat. "Are we holding a vigil? Is he...dying?" She could barely whisper the last word.

"Have ye told him yet?"

"What?"

"Have ye told him how much ye love him?"

"Oh, sweet Lord." Shanley didn't attempt to hold back the tears that spilled over her cheeks. "I'm going to lose him. Just when I finally found him."

"Near as I can tell, he ingested a bit o' the Morhaus's putrid breath. Not enough tae kill him, or he'd already be dead. But enough that his body needs time tae process it." She sipped her tea. "The healin' chant I gave him will help." Smiling over the rim of her mug, she added, "As will tellin' him what ye feel."

For long seconds, Shanley processed Saraid's words. Mainly the ones about Alaisdair not dying.

"Like Tristan all those years ago fighting the Morhaus to save his lady's legacy, Alaisdair has fought a mighty battle fer ye. Like Isolde did fer Tristan, it is up tae ye tae heal him. Talk tae him. Tell him how ye feel. Yer story still has a chance at a happy endin'." Saraid rocked back into the chair and returned her attention to her tea.

Shanley unfolded herself from the heap in which she'd landed on the floor and moved to the bed. Carefully arranging herself next to Alaisdair, she lay her head on his pillow and her hand over his heart. Strangely, she felt no embarrassment at having an audience for so intimate a moment as she set her lips on Alaisdair's ear. "I first fell in love with you in dreams. I fell in love with you again in this very bed. And again when you held me in the training room after my first prophecy." She smoothed her hand over the warm skin of his chest. "Then you went to battle for my niece and for me, and I fell even more in love with you. Finally, you vanquished a demon from my past. In Tristan's story, Andred killed him, finishing what King Mark started. When you killed Logan, you changed the story."

Leaning up on her elbow, she stared down into the still face of the only man she would ever love. With her forefinger, she traced the contours of his forehead, his strong high cheekbones, the slope of his nose that canted slightly to the left, a legacy of some long-ago injury. Finally, she drew her finger over his lips before lowering her mouth to his, kissing him gently.

When she tried to lift her head, Alaisdair's hand shot up and tangled in her hair as he held her to him. Opening his lips beneath hers, he pulled her into an inferno of desire before she could even react. Somewhere in the distance, she heard the snick of a door closing, and then all she could hear were Alaisdair's groans of pleasure—and pain.

Realizing he'd dragged her up onto his chest, Shanley pulled away.

"Lassie, where dae ye think ye're goin'?"

Alaisdair tried to pull her back to her place atop his chest, but still weak from the Morhaus's poison and his last battle with Logan Malo, he couldn't match Shanley's determination to give him space to breathe.

"You're awake. Oh, Alaisdair, you're awake." She smiled at him through a veil of happy tears.

"O' course I'm awake. Why are ye cryin', Shan?"

The concern and genuine confusion she heard in his voice told her more than anything how grave his injuries were.

"You've been out cold and unresponsive for hours, Alaisdair. I-I didn't know if you'd live—"

New tears rained down her face.

With effort, he reached across his body to thumb away her sorrow. "I dreamed ye told me ye loved me."

"I did tell you I love you." She turned her face into his palm and kissed him. "I love you so much." Covering his hand with hers, she held it to her face. "I finally found you—or you discovered me. Either way, I've been waiting for you for so long, and the thought of losing you now—" Staring deep into the whisky-colored eyes she knew she'd see in her dreams for the rest of her life, she said, "Alaisdair, in such a short time, you've become everything to me."

"And ye're everythin' tae me, Shanley." With a grunt of pain, he rolled to face her. "Though I'd rather spend many pleasurable decades with ye, lass, ye have tae know I'd die fer ye."

She closed her eyes tight and pulled him close, letting him feel her heart beating in her chest for him even as she needed the steady rhythms of his heart beating against her. They held each other, locked in their embrace while time waited before a quiet knock at the bedroom door interrupted them.

Saraid poked her head in and said, "Hamish says ye're needed at the ceilidh. Sooner rather than later."

Shanley sat up. "Isn't the ceilidh over? What time is it?"

"The battle and its aftermath occurred in a parallel time and place. Ye know that."

She ducked her head at Saraid's scolding tone. "What seems hours tae ye passed in minutes in the civilian world. If ye hurry, ye'll barely be late fer the ritual tae bind the Conlan heir tae her home—and tae her warrior."

Beside her, Alaisdair groaned. "The Morhaus and my auld

nemesis Logan Malo dinnae succeed in killin' me, but dancin' that reel fer the ritual might."

Saraid rolled her eyes. "It's unbecomin' fer a warrior tae whine, Alaisdair. Now clean yerselves up and hightail it tae the manor. Ye have about ten minutes in civilian time."

On that parting note, Saraid left them and didn't bother to close the bedroom door behind her.

CHAPTER TWENTY

ARRIORS AND CIVILIAN men staggered back into the brightly lit ballroom shortly after midnight. The supper the ladies set out on the buffet along the wall opposite the dais lured revelers who had successfully "secured" the grounds of the manor. Since they'd drunk several flasks of Hamish's whisky during their lark, the civilians took no notice of the way warriors occasionally winced or grimaced when someone clapped one on the back or bumped him on the shoulder as the party returned to full strength.

Shanley and Alaisdair were the first of the warriors to succumb to the effects of bending time and space. Fighting a battle for half of the night while only an hour ticked by on the civilian clock had tired them almost past endurance. Though he had superhuman healing abilities, the bruising Alaisdair sustained and the ingestion of the Morhaus's contagion demanded he rest as he took a seat at one of the round tables ringing the oak dancefloor.

Shanley flinched every time Alaisdair did. Resting a hand on each of their shoulders, Hamish said, "Donnae ye worry about him, lass. Alaisdair's tough. Yer night willnae be ruined." His wink blushed Shanley's cheeks scarlet.

"I was *not* worried about later Hamish Buchanan. If you saw Alaisdair's bruises, you'd know why I'm worried. He needs to go to a hospital and have his ribs checked out."

Alaisdair glared at her indignant tone. The two of them had spent a good deal of the time it took them to clean up for the ceilidh arguing that very point.

"Och, lass. Between Saraid's druidic help and yer warrior's ability tae heal himself, Alaisdair will be good as new before the evenin's done. Nae need fer any civilian doctors." Hamish patted her shoulder in a grandfatherly way. "No' even the best o' them can dae what a skilled druid is capable o' daein'. Ye know that."

"Does that mean Finn will be able to come out of his room before the ceilidh is over?" she asked hopefully.

Hamish sobered in a second. "Finn's wound is grave, lass. Either Morgan enchanted the rogue's sword, or he treated it with some sort o' poison we havnae seen." He pressed her shoulder, holding her down when she tried to rise. "Nae lass, ye cannae go tae him now."

Shanley glared at him.

"Donnae give me that look," Hamish warned. "I'm no' bein' callous. My druid friends are daein' everythin' they can tae help him, but his wound is serious and no' respondin' tae the antivenins they've tried so far. Ye'll be in the way if ye go tae him." His tone was kindly but resolute. "He doesnae want any o' his girls seein' him as he is right now."

Alaisdair slipped an arm around her waist and pulled her close. His bruises radiated heat through the bandages she'd wrapped tightly around his midsection, giving her something else to worry about while Hamish stood in front of the band on the dais to call out another reel. Having completed the ritual handfasting of Rio, the "King Stag" to Ceri, the Conlan heir, the Sheridans and Conlans were to lead the assembly in a series of reels. Every time Hamish called another dance, Alaisdair groaned.

Smiling grimly at her, he rose and took his place across from her for the final reel required of them for the evening. Though he may have hidden it well from the others, Shanley could see the lines of pain bracketing his lips and caught the hissing in of air as he panted through the intricate steps. When the last notes of the bagpipes faded away into the knot patterns plastered into the high ceiling of the ballroom, Alaisdair dropped with a thump onto a nearby chair.

Without missing a beat, Owen Sheridan shoved a dram of Hamish's best whisky into Alaisdair's hand. As she watched him toss the shot back, Shanley thought her warrior didn't even taste the fiery liquid as it burned its way down his throat.

Slamming the shot glass down on the tabletop, Alaisdair declared, "That's it fer me, lads. Time tae call it a night."

At his pronouncement, Shanley stood gracefully from her chair and waited for him to stand, knowing instinctively he'd want no public help from her. Alaisdair pushed himself up and wrapped his arm around her. "Let's go, lass."

Several of the local civilians gave Alaisdair a hard time as they made their way through the throng filling the ballroom in the wee hours of the morning. Good-naturedly, he fielded their ribald jabs but didn't pause in his singular mission of taking the two of them to Shanley's room.

As they descended the stairs to the second floor, Alaisdair leaned heavily on her. She didn't think he realized how much of his weight she bore as they walked the short distance from the stairs to her door. It was a task she was more than up to. Her struggle was with his pain.

Inside the safe confines of her room, he locked the door and turned to her.

"Shan, I know I promised ye another night like last night, but—"

She didn't let him finish. "We are going to go to bed to sleep,

Alaisdair Graham. There will be no shenanigans until you're well and truly healed. Is that understood?"

Wrapping her arms carefully around him, she rested her cheek on his chest. "I can never thank you enough for everything you've done for Ceri and me tonight. And all the years you lived here and took care of our ancestral home."

"The prize is worth it."

She smiled back the tears threatening to fall once again. *Honestly, when did you become so weepy, Shanley Elspeth Conlan?*

A discreet knock at the door interrupted them.

"Who the hell?"

She disengaged herself from Alaisdair's embrace and unlocked the door. "Thank you, Saraid. I appreciate this."

The old woman nodded and headed back upstairs.

"You were expectin' her?"

"She said she had a potion to combat the dregs of the Morhaus's breath you still hold inside you."

Alaisdair ran a hand over his face. "Ye weren't plannin' on a pleasurable end tae this evenin' were ye Shan?"

It was all Shanley could do not to stomp her foot. "Alaisdair Graham, you've proved beyond any doubt how strong and powerful you are. You bested the Morhaus for crying out loud. But you've sustained an injury that would have killed a lesser man. You need rest."

After she set the mug of Saraid's healing concoction on the bureau, she turned back to Alaisdair and began to help him divest himself of his kilt. As they worked together to undress him, he grinned at her. "Is this the way it's goin' tae be between us then?"

She quirked a brow as she folded his plaid and laid it across the chair.

"Ye plan tae boss me often, dae ye?"

Trying not to jostle his torso, she helped him pull off his kilt shirt. "Only if you insist on trying to be Superman all the time."

Standing before her in nothing but his kilt socks and shoes, bandages ringing his torso, he smiled the first genuine smile she'd seen on his face since late afternoon when they'd lost themselves in each other in the sitting room. "Havnae ye figured it out yet, lass? When I'm with ye, I *am* Superman." He pulled her to him and held her close.

Even through the layers of her kilt and plaid, Shanley felt the stirrings of Alaisdair's desire against her belly. As much as she wanted to go there with him, she knew he needed sleep.

"When the sun's up, I imagine you will be too." She smirked impishly up at him. "But tonight, you sleep."

"Shan—" There wasn't much fire in Alaisdair's warning as she stepped away from him to retrieve the drink.

Gifting her a dubious look, he sniffed Saraid's potion before downing it in one gulp. She watched in fascination as his Adam's apple worked while the sleeping draught slid down his throat. The sight left her tingling low in her belly, and she wished for a different ending to their night. Instead, she took the mug from him, turned down the bed, and helped him into it.

"At least let me watch ye undress, Shanley, since it's all I'm goin' tae get taenight."

His heavy eyelids couldn't conceal the banked desire she saw in their whisky-colored depths. Against her better judgment, she stood beside the bed and unwound her plaid and tartan, carefully folding and laying the clothing over Alaisdair's on the chair. She kept her eyes on his as she unbuttoned her blouse and let it fall from her shoulders to catch at her wrists before pooling at her feet on the floor. His lips curved as she stood before him in her socks and lacy bra, then his eyes closed, and his breathing evened out.

Shanley couldn't decide if she was grateful or frustrated. Puffing out a breath, she finished undressing, doused the light, and climbed into bed, spooning herself around her warrior.

CHAPTER TWENTY-ONE

THE DAY OF Finn Daly's memorial dawned so clear and blue, it almost hurt to look up at the sky. The families gathered in the middle of the knot gardens in front of the manor for the service. After Hamish finished the druidic burial chant, each of Finn's "girls" said a few words. As he held Shanley tightly against his side, Alaisdair shared the pain in her heart at losing the old warrior. It seemed the man held a special place in the collective love of the entire Sheridan family, which made his passing especially difficult. Alyssa and Rowan Sheridan insisted on taking Finn's ashes home with them to scatter over his talisman's grave as he'd requested.

During the somber celebratory brunch following the ritual, Owen Sheridan made his way to Alaisdair.

"I understand you haven't left the manor grounds much these last thirteen years."

"That's true enough. I'm lookin' forward tae daein' a little travelin' now that I've found Shanley," Alaisdair said as he added sausages to his plate.

"Ceri says you rebuilt the cottage, including the plumbing and the wiring."

"I did." He stopped adding food to his plate and gave the other man his full attention.

"Since Rio needs to stay here with Ceri for at least the next year, we're going to be short a man at our security firm back home in Montana." He gave Alaisdair a sly glance. "In the same town where Shanley lives."

Owen casually slid three fried eggs onto his plate and waited.

"Are ye offerin' me a job?"

"If you're interested. We could use a man like you, and the opportunity might solve one or two of your personal problems." Owen smirked at him, and Alaisdair burst out laughing.

"Aye, man, it might at that."

"That mean you're interested?"

"Absolutely."

They set their plates on the buffet and shook on their new arrangement.

"What were you and Owen laughing about?" Shanley asked when he joined her on the bench at the long dining table.

"My new job."

"What job?" The alarm on her pretty features was almost comical.

"The one I took in some place in America called Montana."

Her eyes saucered while her mouth executed a decent imitation of a fish. Taking pity on her, Alaisdair cupped her jaw and kissed the side of her gaping mouth. Whispering against her lips, he added, "Hope ye're interested in a roommate."

She pushed away and stared at him for too long. As he started to wonder if he'd been hasty about accepting Owen's offer, she grabbed the front of his shirt with both hands, hauled him in and kissed him until he saw stars.

When they came up for air, she smiled at him while tears shimmered in her forest green eyes.

"I take it ye like the plan, lass," he said, smiling back at her.

"It certainly takes care of those pesky obstacles."

He raised a brow.

"Ocean, continent. Little things really."

It was his turn to pull her in and kiss her senseless.

The ringing silence in the room brought him back to himself. Reluctantly, he ended the kiss, though his hands remained on Shanley as they looked around at the expectant faces staring at the two of them.

"Somethin' tae celebrate, lad?" Hamish asked.

"Looks like I'll be followin' this woman home."

From across the table, Owen said, "I take it my offer meets with your approval, Shanley?"

She slipped her arm around Alaisdair's waist, leaned her head on his shoulder, and smiled at Owen. "Thank you."

The table erupted in cheers and congratulations, the perfect antidote to the sadness of Finn's death. Before long, talk turned to boasting about the comeuppance the warriors had once again given the Morrigan and travel plans for their return to America.

"Nae doubt it's goin' tae be different around the manor," Hamish said as he stood beside Alaisdair in the waiting area of Inverness's small airport.

"Ye'll have yer hands full with Rio, that's fer sure." Alaisdair grinned.

"He's a good lad. All the Sheridans are good people. I'm glad tae know 'em and glad tae have the services o' their greatest warrior."

Alaisdair rocked on his heels.

"But lad, we've been through much taegether, ye and I, and

I'd be lyin' if I dinnae admit I'm goin' tae miss ye. Even if that boy can play any chess"—he glanced in Rio's direction—"I doubt he'll want tae give up his evenin's with our bonny Ceri tae entertain an auld druid." His eyes twinkled. "No' that I'd have any better luck with ye if Shanley and ye stayed at the manor."

"I've nae doubt ye'll find somethin' tae keep ye busy. Meddlin', I expect."

Hamish grinned. "Ye might ask Shanley about that."

Alaisdair quirked a brow.

The boarding call crackled over the PA, and Alaisdair knew they'd prolonged their parting as long as possible. He hugged the old man close. "Ye've been as much a father tae me as my own da. I owe ye everythin', auld man."

Hamish hugged him back hard. "I'm goin' tae miss ye, lad. But I always knew this day would come. Ye deserve yer happiness."

Alaisdair nodded.

"And ye'll be back. Probably more often than ye think."

Alaisdair stepped back, a smile curving his lips. "Already started with the meddlin' have ye?"

Hamish winked and turned his attention to Shanley who wiped tears from her eyes as she let go of Ceri. "Take care o' him, lass. With as hardheaded as he can be sometimes, he's goin' tae need ye tae watch out fer him." He kissed his cousin and pushed her toward Alaisdair. "'Tis a grand adventure the twa o' ye are startin'. Ye can tell us all about it when we see ye at Christmas."

"Indeed, Hamish." Alaisdair draped his arm over Shanley's shoulder and brushed a kiss over her temple. Staring deep into the forests of her eyes, he said, "Ye are most definitely the grandest adventure of my life. I love ye, Shanley Conlan. Now show me yer America."

Thank you for reading *Prophetess*. Turn the page for a preview of *Bard*, Book Four in the Talisman Series coming July 2020.

CHAPTER ONE

THE BELL OVER the outer door to her office chimed, shattering Fallon Graham's concentration on her screen.

"Is this where I can buy season tickets for football?" asked the gorgeous blond man on the other side of her desk.

A scene flashed through her mind as Fallon stared at him, transfixed.

He rested his forearms on the counter, and she blinked back into the moment. "I'm sorry. Maybe you didn't hear me." His smile mesmerized her. "I was wondering if I could buy season tickets here." The melodious baritone of his voice washed over her, rippling through her chest.

Her face heated. Clearing her throat, she tried to regain control of herself. "Um, yes. Yes, it is. How many tickets do you need, and in which section of the stadium would you like to sit?" Attempting to recover some professionalism, she pulled her computer closer and called up the requisite ticket program. With the receptionist out on her break, it fell to Fallon to cover general foot traffic and telephone calls.

Normally, selling game tickets to a hot guy was ample

compensation for doing extra work. Dealing with this particular man was more like hazardous duty. That he was a warrior she had no doubt. No way could he look like the man whose fate had just slashed through her mind and not be a warrior. After all, she wouldn't have had a premonition about a civilian, would she? What she couldn't understand was why his story raced through her head at all, specifically his death. Unable to stop herself, she sneaked another peek over the top of her computer.

"I'll need three—make that four seats in the upper deck above the student section if you have them. Maybe I'll have a date when the season starts." He winked.

Judging from his height and the breadth of his shoulders, the man could know a thing or two about football from playing the game. Or maybe he put an inordinate amount of time into warrior training. Either way, he was sex on a stick. Certainly, he wasn't coming on to her, was he? "Let me see what we have," she said as she studiously applied herself to fulfilling his request. Those shoulders and the fact that she'd just seen them naked kept distracting her though, and she struggled to keep her mind on her task.

While the woman studied her computer, Seamus Lochlann studied—Fallon Graham, according to the nameplate on her desk. He was used to having an effect on women, especially civilians. The pretty blush on this lady's face told him she wasn't immune to him. *Damn, she's hot. She might not be my usual preference— tall, leggy, blonde—but this woman is gorgeous. What color are her eyes—Green? Blue? Golden brown? And that mouth. I could kiss that for hours.*

The flustered way she acted in his presence amused him. He grinned broadly at her when she sneaked a glance at him, an action that deepened her blush and caused her to lose her place in her task. *Must not laugh*, he admonished himself at the way he so obviously got to her.

When she found four seats together in the upper deck of the stadium, she swung her computer around to let him see his choices.

"I'll take the seats in this section here," he indicated with his index finger brushing the screen of her computer, and she sucked in a breath.

Seamus liked that she sounded unsteady when she said, "Super. Let me grab those for you."

She walked over to the other desk in the office to grab the tickets, giving him an uninterrupted view of her shapely athletic legs—beneath the fitted pencil skirt she wore—to her tight, rounded ass and slim waist. Thick auburn hair cascaded down her perfectly curved back. Involuntarily, he flexed his hands. *What I wouldn't give to plunge my fingers into all that hair.* When she returned with the tickets, he appreciated how her blouse didn't hide her generous curves. The way she moved radiated sexy. *Yeah, I'd like to know Fallon Graham a whole lot better.*

As she handed him the tickets, he automatically attempted his sign on her, but instead of deftly tracing his Celtic trinity knot on her wrist as he took the tickets from her, a piece of armor masquerading as a bracelet stymied him. She frowned at him and jerked her hand behind her back.

"Anything else I can do for you?" she asked, her tone professionally polite.

He didn't miss that she pulled her hands behind her back. "Yeah. Will you show me your bracelet?"

She blinked at him and lifted her hand for him to inspect her jewelry.

"Interesting piece of armor you're wearing there. A remnant from your Wonder Woman costume at Halloween?" he teased.

"Something like that."

Then he noticed the triskele. *If this woman is a talisman, I can't ask her outright to remove her bracelet. I need to find another way to try my sign on her.*

"So, Fallon—that's your name, right?"

"I see you can read," she said with half a grin.

He didn't miss a beat. "One of my many talents." Taking a step closer to her, he said, "I'm Seamus Lochlann, and I was wondering what you're doing tonight."

ACKNOWLEDGEMENTS

THOUGH WRITING IS a solitary experience, it takes a team to put a book out into the world. I'm fortunate to have a stellar team, and I'm truly grateful to all of you.

Coleene Torgerson, the early drafts of this story were imbedded in *Warrior* when it was a sprawling 140,000 word mess. You cheerfully read it anyway and gave me encouraging feedback. This is why I love you so much. You always see the positive and give me hope that I'm on the right track. I'm exceptionally lucky you've been in my life for nearly all of it.

You ask me regularly if I have a book for you, Bri Brasher. Your willingness to read the early drafts and your genuine enthusiasm for the work makes me want to write the best story I can so as not to disappoint you. Your insights on this one reiterated my thoughts and helped me make the choices I knew in my heart I needed to make. Thank you.

My writing coterie (a pretty word for beautiful people), your continuous encouragement, examples, and input on my writing journey have made me a better writer. Angela Forester, Angie Randak, Sue Ellen Turnbull, and Alison Packard, I value each of you so much. Thank you especially, Sue Ellen, for your insights on this story. Our national group may have imploded and restructured, but I will be forever grateful to have met you ladies because of that group.

These books would not exist if not for the expertise of my editor, Nikki Busch. With every story we work on together, you make me better. Perhaps someday we'll be able to hit a rock concert together.

I have a superstar webmaster who makes me look awesome online. Thank you so much, Levi Meyer, for your professionalism, insights, and ideas. I always look forward to coffee, lunch, or a beer with you. (And yes, I will regret your Advanced Comp. grade to the end of my days. So glad you've forgiven me—mostly.)

Maria at Steamy Designs, your gorgeous covers make my books look awesome. Thank you. Chrissy at Damonza, you give my books extra polish and shine with your perfect formatting. Thank you both for your excellent work on this series.

To the Gorgeous Goddesses: Lori Hodges, Joni Blood, Anita Daubert, and Brenda Emerick, our dinners together are a highlight of my month. Thanks for all the laughs, the drinks, the introductions to all the fun places to eat in the Magic City, and your on-going support. I'm so happy you like my books.

Finally, my story would be incomplete without my wonderful guys. Grady, Austin, Trey—I love you with my whole self. You, my husband and sons, are my world.

To my Warriors, the awesome readers who enjoy and share my books, THANK YOU. Because of you, I get to pursue this storytelling life I've always dreamed of. Reviews help writers connect with new readers. If you would be so kind as to leave a review wherever you like to share your reading experiences, I'd appreciate it. You can find me on GoodReads, BookBub, Barnes & Noble, and Amazon. If you want to know what's next in the

Talisman Series, please follow me on Instagram @tamstales32, on my website: www.tamderudderjackson.com, or on Facebook at Tam DeRudder Jackson. If you're interested in increasing your luck, check out my blog: Try Thirty New Things on WordPress. Let's grow together.

ABOUT THE AUTHOR

TAM DERUDDER JACKSON is the author of the Talisman Series. In her previous career, Tam was an award-winning high school English teacher. Today, she's living her dream of writing novels. When she's not writing, she's reading all the books or carving turns on the ski runs in the mountains near her home in northwest Wyoming or traveling to places on her ever-expanding bucket list. Her two grown sons are the joys of her life, and she likes supporting her husband's old car habit. If you ever see her holding a map, do her a favor and point her in the right direction. Navigation has never been her strong suit.

www.ingramcontent.com/pod-product-compliance
Lightning Source LLC
Chambersburg PA
CBHW021200110726
47900CB00002B/660

* 9 7 8 1 7 3 4 2 6 6 6 4 1 *